It was a stupid, insane, suicidal idea. Which makes it quite hard to explain why I decided to help. I guess it boils down to this. Charlie was my best friend. I missed him. And I couldn't think of anything better to do. Really stupid reasons which were never going to impress the police, the headmistress or my parents.

Looking back, I reckon this was the moment when my whole life started to go pear-shaped.

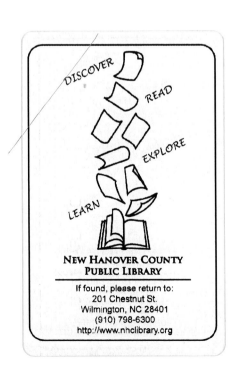

DISCOVER READ EXPLORE LEARN

**NEW HANOVER COUNTY
PUBLIC LIBRARY**

If found, please return to:
201 Chestnut St.
Wilmington, NC 28401
(910) 798-6300
http://www.nhclibrary.org

boom!

Also by Mark Haddon

The Curious Incident of the Dog in the Night-time

# boom!

(or 70,000 light years)

## mark haddon

David Fickling Books

OXFORD · NEW YORK

A DAVID FICKLING BOOK

Published in the United States by David Fickling Books,
an imprint of Random House Children's Books,
a division of Random House, Inc., New York.
An earlier version of this text was published in
a different form in Great Britain as *Gridzbi Spudvetch!*
by Walker Books, London, in 1992.
This illustrated edition was originally published
in Great Britain by David Fickling Books,
an imprint of Random House Children's Books,
a division of the Random House Group Ltd., London, in 2009.

David Fickling Books and the colophon are trademarks
of David Fickling.

Visit us on the Web! www.randomhouse.com/kids

Educators and librarians, for a variety of teaching tools,
visit us at www.randomhouse.com/teachers

Library of Congress Cataloging-in-Publication Data
is available upon request.
ISBN 978-0-385-75187-2 (trade) — ISBN 978-0-385-75188-9 (lib. bdg.)
— ISBN 978-0-375-89364-3 (e-book)

Printed in the United States of America
May 2010
10 9 8 7 6 5 4 3 2 1

First U.S. Edition

This book is dedicated to Miss Williams and Lilac Four. They are . . . Zack, Kiran, George H., George, Kareem, Simon, Michael, Filipp, Alek, Laurence, Tim S., Henry, Fangze, Tim W., Megan, Anna, Lily, Lottie, Lubna, Clara, Charlie, Elsie, Lola and Jessica.

I also owe a big thank-you to Anna Johnson for typing out the entire text and putting it onto disk so that I could edit it properly.

# foreword

*This book was first published in 1992 under the title Gridzbi Spudvetch! It was a ridiculous thing to call a book. No one knew how to pronounce it. And no one knew what it meant until they'd read the story. As a result only twenty-three people bought the book. Actually, that's an exaggeration, but not much. It rapidly went out of print.*

*It would have stayed out of print, but over the years a string of people got in touch to say how much they loved the book. On several occasions my publishers asked whether I wanted to update it for a new edition.*

*It certainly needed updating. It was full of references to floppy disks and Walkmans and cassette players. But it needed more than that. There were numerous little holes in the plot. Much of the writing was clumsy. And I couldn't read it without thinking Ouch! on almost every page. A new edition would need major rewriting. Rewriting takes time, however. And I didn't have much.*

*Towards the end of 2007 I got a letter from SS Philip and James Primary School (aka Phil and Jim's) in Oxford. Alison Williams said that she had been reading the book to her pupils for years and it was always guaranteed to entertain them. To prove her point she included a sheaf of letters from her Lilac Four class, and they were kind and funny and very complimentary.*

*I was finally persuaded. I put aside some time and returned to Gridzbi Spudvetch! armed with a scalpel and a red pencil. I cut large sections and added new ones. By the end of the process I'd changed pretty much every sentence in the book one way or another.*

*I'd also come up with a new title. It means something even if you haven't read the story. And everyone can pronounce it.*

# 1

# helicopter sandwich

I was on the balcony eating a sandwich. Red Leicester and gooseberry jam. I took a mouthful and chewed. It was good but not a patch on strawberry jam and Cheddar. That was my best yet.

I spent a lot of time on the balcony. The flat was tiny. Sometimes it felt like living in a submarine. But the balcony was amazing. The wind. The sky. The light. You could see the 747s circling slowly in the stack, waiting for a space on the runway at Heathrow. You could watch police cars weaving their way through the tiny streets like toys, their sirens whooping.

You could see the park too. And on this particular morning you could see, in the middle of the huge expanse of grass, a solitary man holding a metal box in his hands. Buzzing high above his head you could just make out a model helicopter, banking and swerving like a dragonfly.

Dad has always been crazy about models. Trains,

planes, tanks, vintage cars. But after he lost his job at the car factory it became the biggest thing in his life. To be fair, he was brilliant. Give him a brick and a rubber band and he'd have it looping the loop before you could say, 'Chocks away!' But it didn't seem right somehow. It was a hobby for little boys and weird blokes who still lived with their mums.

A flock of pigeons clattered past and I heard the sound of a familiar motorbike engine. I looked down and saw Craterface's large black Moto Guzzi turn into the estate car park. My darling sister, Becky, was on the seat behind him, a grimy leather jacket over her school uniform.

She was sixteen. I could remember the time, only a couple of years back, when she tied her hair in bunches and had pony posters on her bedroom wall. Then something went badly wrong in her brain. She started listening to death metal and stopped washing her armpits.

She met Craterface at a gig six months ago. He was nineteen. He had long greasy hair and enormous sideburns with bits of breakfast stuck in them. When he was younger he had spots. They'd gone now, but they'd left these holes behind. Hence the nickname. His face looked like the surface of the moon.

He had the brain of a toilet brush. Mum, Dad and I were in complete agreement about this. Becky, however, thought he was God's Gift to Women. Why she fancied him, I haven't a clue. Perhaps he was the only person who could stand her armpits.

The bike rumbled to a halt ten storeys below and I experienced a moment of utter madness. Without thinking, I peeled off half my sandwich, leaned out and let go. I realized almost immediately that I had done a very, very stupid thing. If it hit them I would be murdered.

The slice wobbled and flipped and veered left and veered right. Craterface turned off the engine, got off the bike, removed his helmet and looked up towards the flat. I felt sick.

The slice hit him in the face and stuck, jammy side down. For a couple of seconds Craterface just stood there, absolutely motionless, the slice of bread sitting there like a face pack. Becky was standing beside him, looking up at me. She was not a happy bunny.

Now, normally you can't hear much from the balcony, on account of the traffic. But when Craterface tore the sandwich off and roared, I think they probably heard him in Japan.

He stormed towards the doors but Becky grabbed his wrist and dragged him to a halt. She wasn't worried about me. She'd have quite liked him to kill me. Just not in the flat. Because that would get her into trouble.

Craterface finally saw sense. He waved his fist and shouted, 'You're dead, scum!' climbed onto the Moto Guzzi and thundered away in a gust of dirty grey fumes.

Becky turned and strode towards the door. I looked down at the rest of my sandwich and realized that I no longer felt very hungry. There was no one in the car park now so I dropped this half too, and watched it wobble and flip and veer and land neatly beside the first slice.

At which point the balcony door was kicked open. I said, 'It was an accident,' but Becky screamed, 'You little toad!' and hit me really hard on the side of the head, which hurt quite a lot.

For a couple of seconds everything went double. I could see two Beckys and two balconies and two rubber plants. I didn't cry, because if I cried Becky would call me a baby, which was worse than being hit. So I hung onto the rail until the pain died down and there was only one Becky again.

'What did you do that for?' I asked. 'It didn't land on you. It landed on Craterface.'

She narrowed her eyes. 'You are so lucky he didn't come up here and hit you himself.'

She was right, really. Craterface had a black belt in kung fu. He could kill people with his ears.

'And another thing,' she hissed. 'His name is Terry.'

'Actually, I've heard his name is Florian. He just pretends to be called Terry.' I stepped backwards to avoid the second punch but it never came. Instead, Becky went very quiet, leaned against the railing and nodded slowly. 'That reminds me,' she said, in a sinisterly pleasant way. 'There's something I've been meaning to tell you.'

'What?'

'Amy and I were in the staff room the other day, talking to Mrs Cottingham.' Becky took a packet of cigarettes from the pocket of her leather jacket and lit one very slowly, as if she were in a black and white film.

'Smoking's bad for you,' I said.

'Shut your ugly mouth and listen.' She sucked in a lungful of smoke. 'We overheard Mr Kidd talking about you.'

'What was he saying?'

'Bad things, Jimbo. Bad things.' This had to be a

wind-up. But she wasn't smiling. And it didn't sound like a wind-up.

'What bad things?' I pulled nervously at the rubber plant and one of the leaves came off in my hand.

'That you're lazy. That you're a nuisance.'

'You're lying.' I slid the leaf of the rubber plant down the back of the deckchair.

'According to Mr Kidd your work is rubbish. According to Mr Kidd – and this is the really good bit – they're thinking of sending you to that school in Fenham. You know, that special place for kids with problems.' She blew a smoke ring.

'That's not true.' I felt giddy. 'They can't do that.'

'Apparently they can.' She nodded. 'Jodie's brother got sent there.' She stubbed out her cigarette in one of the plant pots and flicked it over the railing. 'Jodie said it's like a zoo. You know, bars on the windows, kids howling all the time.'

The glass door slid open and Mum stepped out onto the balcony holding one of her shoes in her hand.

'Hello, you two,' she said, wiping the sole of the shoe with a wet cloth. 'Honestly, the mess on this estate. I just trod on a half-eaten sandwich, of all things.'

I turned round so that Mum couldn't see my face, and as I did so I saw, in the distance, Dad's helicopter clip the top of a tree, burst into flames, spiral downwards and land in the gravel of the dog toilet, scaring the living daylights out of a large Dalmatian.

Dad threw the control box to the ground and lay face-down on the grass, hammering it with his fists.

# 2

# bad things

The atmosphere over supper was not good.

Becky told Mum it was my sandwich. Mum tore me off a strip for wasting good food. Becky said wasting food wasn't the point. The point was dropping it on Craterface. So Mum said you could drop a piano on Craterface and it wouldn't make much difference. At this point Becky swore and stomped off to her room.

To make matters worse, Dad had forgotten to take the chicken out of the freezer. He'd forgotten to buy more washing-up liquid. And he was sulking about his helicopter, which was now lying in the hall, burned, broken and covered with bits of gravel and dog-do.

'It's only a toy,' insisted Mum, halfway through yesterday's left-over lasagne.

'It. Is. Not. A. Toy!' shouted Dad.

It got very noisy at this point, so I slipped off to the kitchen and earned some Brownie points by doing the washing up. Unfortunately I had to use the lemon-flavoured soap from the bathroom, which made everything taste funny for the next few days.

When I'd finished I went out onto the balcony for some peace and quiet. Dad joined me five minutes later. He leaned on the railings beside me and gazed out into the darkness.

'Life's a cowpat sandwich, Jimbo,' he sighed, 'with very thin bread and a lot of filling.'

'You can mend the helicopter,' I reassured him.

'Yeah,' he said, 'I know.' Then he went all sad and silent. I knew what was going to happen. We were going to have one of those conversations about how he didn't feel like a real man any more. I wouldn't know what to say. He'd tell me to work hard at school, because I needed good exam results so I could get a job because there was nothing worse than being unemployed.

I didn't want one of those conversations. Not now. I particularly didn't want to think about school and exam results and jobs.

'I don't know how you lot put up with me,' he ploughed on mournfully. 'I can't cook. I can't clean. I forget the shopping and I mope around the house all day.'

'You'll get another job,' I said. 'And anyway, I think lasagne's much nicer than chicken.'

He laughed and we stared out into the dark. After a

minute or two I found myself thinking about the school thing. Mr Kidd and Fenham and the bars on the windows and the howling. 'Dad?' I asked.

'What?'

I wanted to tell him how worried I was. But it didn't seem fair. He had enough on his plate. And the possibility that I was going to be expelled wasn't going to cheer him up.

'Oh, nothing,' I said vaguely. 'Look, I've got to go and do some stuff.'

'Sure.' He ruffled my hair. 'Catch you later, pardner.'

I grabbed my jacket, slipped out of the front door and headed down the stairs.

Becky had to be lying. If she was telling the truth then she was being helpful. Warning me what was going on. Giving me a chance to pull my socks up. And Becky had never been helpful to me in her entire life.

Plus, she had a Nobel Prize in winding people up. Last year I went into hospital to have a squint in my eye put right. Before I went in, she kept telling me about all the things that could go wrong. The anaesthetic might not work. I'd be lying there, wide awake, unable to move, watching them cutting my eye open. They might give me too little oxygen and damage my brain. They might mix me up with someone else and amputate my leg.

I was so terrified that I was wheeled into the operating theatre holding a large piece of paper on which I'd written: PLEASE MAKE SURE I AM PROPERLY ASLEEP. The nurses thought it was hilarious.

On the other hand, I did muck about in class. I was in detention every other week. And I was not Albert Einstein.

In fact, getting chucked out of school would be pretty much par for the course. Everything seemed to have gone wrong over the past six months. It wasn't just Dad losing his job. It was Mum getting a job that paid double what he'd ever earned at the car plant. She did a part-time business course at the College of Further Education, came top and ended up with a job at Perkins and Thingamy in town.

So, while Dad slouched around all day feeling sorry for himself, circling job adverts in the paper and gluing bits of balsa wood together, Mum zipped back and forth in her new red Volkswagen, dressed in natty suits and carrying a briefcase with a combination lock.

Some days it seemed as if the whole world had been turned upside down.

boom!

In ten minutes I was standing in front of Charlie's house. It was a big posh job, four storeys, garage, an actual drive. Dr Brooks, Charlie's dad, was a short, wiry man with monumental eyebrows, who spoke as little as possible. He worked as a police surgeon. He was the guy you see on the TV, standing over the dead body, saying, 'He was killed by a blow to the head with a crowbar at approximately four a.m.'

Mrs Brooks, Charlie's mum, was completely different. She was a professional cook who did wedding receptions and conference banquets. She had a kitchen the size of an aircraft hangar and a fridge the size of our flat. She had a temper like a flame-thrower and talked pretty much constantly.

I walked through the gate and up to the front door, wondering why someone had ripped up the flower-bed in front of the lounge window. I was about to ring the bell when I heard a fake owl-hoot from above my head. I looked up and saw Charlie leaning out of his bedroom window. He pressed his finger to his lips and pointed round the side of the house. I kept my trap shut and followed the direction of his finger.

As I stood in the dark passage next to the garage, Charlie's other window creaked open and I saw a rope ladder falling towards me. 'Come up,' whispered Charlie. I started to climb, trying very hard not to fall off or put my foot through a window.

'What's all this about?' I asked, sitting on his bed and getting my breath back.

'I'm grounded,' he explained, rolling the rope ladder back up again. 'Level Ten. No going out. No friends round. No TV. Nothing.'

'What for?'

'I decided it was time I learned to drive,' he said.

'Why?'

'Driving is a very useful skill to have, Jimbo,' he said, turning on the radio to cover the sound of our conversation. 'It seemed like a good idea to start early. So I took the keys from the fruit bowl and got Mum's car out of the garage while she was at the hairdresser's. Did a bit of first gear and reverse up and down the drive. Then it all went a bit pear-shaped.'

'Let me guess,' I said. 'You drove into the flowerbed.'

'Smashed a headlight too,' said Charlie. 'I am seriously not in Mum's good books at the moment.'

boom!

We lay around for half an hour, reading old copies of *Police Surgeon's Weekly* that Charlie had nicked from his dad's study, looking for pictures of really bad industrial accidents. Then I finally got round to telling Charlie what had been bugging me all evening.

'I'm in trouble.'

'Join the club,' he said.

'No,' I insisted. 'I mean *big* trouble.'

'Tell me.'

So I told him. He was always the right person to talk to about stuff like this. He listened properly and thought hard and when he said something it was usually pretty sensible.

Charlie looked like a Victorian chimney sweep – pointy face, beady eyes, hair going in all directions, clothes a couple of sizes too large. Not that you'd really notice him. He didn't say much in class and he avoided fights in the playground. He was the person who is always leaning against a wall somewhere in the background, keeping his eye on things.

'You know something, Jimbo,' he said when I'd finished my story.

'What?'

'You are one gullible prat. If your sister told you that the sky was going to fall down, you'd go round wearing a crash helmet.'

'But . . .' I was feeling embarrassed now. 'It could be true, couldn't it? I mean, it's possible, right?'

'Well,' he said, 'there's only one thing to do. We have to find out what the teachers really think of you.' He wandered over to the far side of the room, shoved the bed aside, lifted a loose floorboard and extracted a small black object from the hole.

'What's that?' I asked.

'A walkie-talkie,' he replied. 'And it's going to solve this problem once and for all.'

'How?' I asked.

Charlie flicked a switch on the walkie-talkie and I heard his mum's voice crackling out of the speaker: '. . . I don't care what you say, that boy has got to learn his lesson. This week he's trying to drive the car. Next week he'll be burning the house down. Now, what do you fancy for supper? I've got some of the trout left over from the Kenyons' wedding. I could rustle up some new potatoes and green beans—'

Charlie flicked the switch off. 'The other one's in the

kitchen, on top of the dresser.' He put the walkie-talkie back under the floorboards. 'I use it to keep in touch with what's going on down there in Parentland. Good, eh?'

'Brilliant,' I said. 'But how is it going to help me?'

'Use your brain, Jimbo,' said Charlie, tapping his forehead. 'We put one in the staff room.'

'Isn't that a bit risky?' I said nervously. Things were bad enough already. If the teachers found me bugging their private conversations I'd be marched out of the school gates and banged up in Fenham before tea time.

'Course it's risky,' said Charlie, shrugging his shoulders. 'It wouldn't be any fun if it wasn't risky.'

I was halfway down the rope ladder when a light came on. There was an ominous thump and I looked up to see Charlie's mum looming out of the staircase window.

She was carrying the secateurs she used for clipping her roses. 'Good evening, Jim.' She smiled down at me. 'And what a pleasant evening it is.'

'Er, yes,' I croaked. 'Very pleasant.'

'Especially for climbing into people's houses uninvited,' she tutted. 'Why, Jim, I might have thought you were a burglar, mightn't I? And if I'd thought you were a burglar, heaven knows what might have happened.'

I clambered down the ladder as fast as I could. It wasn't fast enough. And this is what I mean about the flame-thrower temper. I've seen Charlie's mum throw a breadboard across the kitchen during an argument. She just doesn't operate according to the normal rules of being a grown-up.

I was a couple of metres off the ground when she cut through one of the ropes of the ladder. I lost my footing and found myself dangling upside down. Then she cut the other rope and I hit the gravel, tearing the sleeve of my shirt and scraping the skin off my elbows.

As I ran for the front gate, I could hear her bellowing, 'Charlie . . . ! You get down here right now!' I just hoped she wasn't holding the breadboard.

# 3
# walkie-talkie

**C**harlie had the plan worked out like a bank heist.

He'd pop into the staff room at break and hide the walkie-talkie under a chair. The weekly teachers' meeting began just after the end of school. When the playground was empty we'd slip into the athletics shed and tune in using the second walkie-talkie.

If they said nothing, I was in the clear and we'd fill Becky's bike helmet with mayonnaise. If they mentioned my removal to Fenham, it was time to start doing three hours of homework a night and buying presents for all my teachers.

There were flaws in the plan, obviously. They might have more important things to talk about than me. They might have discussed my removal to Fenham last week. To be honest, I think Charlie was more interested in bugging the staff room than putting my mind at ease.

Worst of all, we might be found by the caretaker. When Mr McLennan caught the Patterson twins in the athletics shed last year he simply pretended he hadn't seen them and locked them in overnight. He was very nearly sacked but the headmistress reckoned it would help cut down vandalism if everyone knew there was a dangerous lunatic looking after the school buildings.

On the other hand, what else could I do? I had no brilliant plan of my own and at least I was doing something positive. Doing something positive, as Mum was always saying, is a jolly good thing. Much better than sitting around all day moping. Like a certain member of our family.

Besides, two people wanted to kill me. A secateur-wielding cook and a kung-fu death metal biker. One lived at Charlie's house and the other spent a great deal of time at our flat. In the greater scheme of things the athletics shed was probably the safest place to be.

I met up with Charlie the following morning at the school gates just before assembly. His right hand was wrapped in a large white bandage, with faint bloodstains seeping through it. A hideous image flashed through my mind.

'Oh my God!' I said. 'She cut your fingers off.'

'What?'

'With the secateurs.'

'No, no, no,' Charlie laughed, shaking his head. 'She's crazy, but she's not that crazy. I tried to escape. I jumped over the window ledge and scrambled down the ladder. I thought I'd come back when she'd cooled off.'

'But she cut the ladder in half.'

'As I discovered.' He held up his wounded hands. 'I landed on a pile of old plant pots.'

'Nasty.'

'It could have been worse,' he said. 'There was a box of garden tools next to the pots.'

We began the morning doing physics with Mr Kosinsky. Mr Kosinsky thought he was very funny. We thought he was a stick insect with weird socks. You could always see his socks because his trousers were too short. This morning they had little pictures of snowmen all over them.

'Ah, you lot,' he said, whisking his jacket off and slipping it over the back of his chair. 'What a treat. Now, what were we doing last time? Was it, by any chance, the role of quarks and gluons in quantum field theory?'

'Gravity, sir,' said Mehmet. 'We were doing gravity.'

'Ah yes, my mistake,' said Mr Kosinsky, easing his lanky body into his seat. 'Now, who can give me a quick résumé of what we were doing on Monday?'

Dennis stuck his hand in the air and started telling everyone about Isaac Newton and escape velocity and why it was so difficult going to the loo in a space-ship.

I looked into Mr Kosinsky's eyes. Did he think I was a brainless nuisance? Had he decided that he couldn't bear teaching me any longer? Was he the sort of man who would want to expel someone?

I glanced over at Megan Shotts. She was sitting in the back row, as per usual, carving chunks out of her desk with a penknife. Megan beat up small boys in the playground. She knocked the wing mirrors off Mrs Benton's car. Last summer she let out the locusts from the biology lab. I found one in my packed lunch. I could be a pain at times, even I knew that. But I couldn't hold a candle to Megan.

# boom!

I glanced in the other direction. Barry Griffin. He'd answered a couple of questions last year, got them wrong, then gone into permanent hibernation. He spent every lesson staring into the distance, motionless and vacant, like someone listening to music on earphones. Except that he didn't have any earphones. What he did have was short legs and very long arms. He looked like prehistoric man. Barry made me look like a guy from NASA.

Why should I get sent to a special school instead of those two? Becky had to be lying.

'Earth calling Jim.'

I looked up to see Mr Kosinsky standing next to my desk.

'Yes?' I said.

'The tides, Jim. What causes the tides?'

'Well . . .' I said, floundering.

Mr Kosinsky bent down and looked into my ear. 'Astonishing. I can see all the way through and out the other side.'

People started to laugh.

'What causes the tides, Jim?' he asked for a second time. 'Is it perhaps the gravitational pull of the sun?'

'It might be,' I said gingerly.

'Or is it perhaps a very large fish called Brian?'

'Probably not,' I said.

'Jim,' he sighed, walking back to the front of the room, 'I sometimes wonder why you bother coming to school at all.'

My heart sank. Perhaps Becky was right after all.

After lunch I lingered by the school secretary's door and watched Charlie do the drop. With the walkie-talkie tucked snugly inside his jacket pocket, he knocked on the door of the staff room. The door opened and Mr Kidd appeared with a mouth full of sausage roll and a copy of *What Car?* in his hand.

Mr Kidd taught art. He wasn't really meant to be a teacher. He looked like he'd wandered into a school some years ago and never quite managed to get out. His tie was always undone, his shirtsleeves were always rolled up and he always had a slightly depressed look on his face. I think he really wanted to be at home watching Sky Sports with a can of lager. On the other hand, he could draw a really good picture of a horse. And horses are seriously difficult.

# boom!

'Excuse me, sir,' said Charlie. 'Do you mind if I come in and have a word?'

'Can't you . . .' Mr Kidd swallowed his mouthful of sausage roll. 'Can't you tell me out here?'

'It's kind of a personal problem,' said Charlie.

'Oh, all right, all right,' agreed Mr Kidd, wafting him inside with his magazine.

A few minutes later Charlie re-emerged into the corridor and grinned at me.

'Did you do it?' I asked.

He slapped an arm round my shoulder as we walked away. 'Sometimes I am so cool I even amaze myself.'

'So what was the personal problem?'

But at this moment the bell rang.

'I'll tell you later,' said Charlie, and we headed back to the classroom.

In the afternoon we did the Industrial Revolution with Mrs Pearce. The spinning jenny. Watt's steam engine. Children being sent down mines. Or rather, that's what everyone else did. Me, I just sat at the back of the

class thinking about getting sent to Fenham and being murdered by Craterface and how going down a mine sounded preferable to both.

At the end of school we hung about for ten minutes or so, then slipped into the athletics shed. Charlie took the second walkie-talkie from his bag and turned it on, and suddenly we were spying on our teachers.

For a couple of minutes it was one of the most exciting things I'd ever done. Over the next quarter of an hour, however, it rapidly became one of the most tedious things I'd ever done. They talked about the £400 they were going to spend on new books for the library. They talked about the fire safety drill. They talked about which contractors they were going to use to re-tarmac the playground. They talked about the secretary leaving to have a baby. They talked about the staff toilet and how it didn't flush properly.

I began to understand why Mr Kosinsky wore weird socks. Choosing what to put on his feet every morning was probably the most thrilling part of his day.

# boom!

'By the way,' said the crackly voice of Mr Kidd over the walkie-talkie, 'Charlie Brooks came to see me at lunch today. You probably saw his bandages.'

There were murmurs around the room.

'Hey, they're talking about you,' I hissed at Charlie.

'Shhhh!' he hissed back.

'Apparently,' continued Mr Kidd, 'he was attacked by the neighbour's dog. Bit of a vicious brute, it seems. The poor boy very nearly lost his fingers. His parents had to rush him to hospital.'

'You what?' I spluttered at Charlie.

Charlie looked very smug indeed.

'So, go easy on him over the next few days,' said Mr Kidd. 'He sounded pretty shaken by the whole affair.'

Grunts of agreement came out of the little black speaker.

I glanced over at Charlie. 'Now that was clever.'

Charlie just smiled at me and said, 'Well, it looks like you're in the clear too.'

'Maybe not,' I said.

'Which is more important?' said Charlie. 'You geting expelled, or the staff toilet not flushing properly? If you were going to be expelled, I think they'd have mentioned it.'

'You're probably right,' I agreed.

'So,' said Charlie, 'when do we put the mayonnaise in Becky's helmet?'

'Now that I think about it, I'm not sure that's a terribly good plan.' I stood up. 'I don't want to wind Craterface up even more.'

In the staff room teachers were scraping their chairs back from the table, filling their briefcases and heading home.

'Give them five minutes to get away,' said Charlie, stretching his legs and yawning. 'Then the coast'll be clear and we can split.'

It was at this point that something very odd happened. I'd picked up the walkie-talkie and was about to turn the thing off when it said, 'Bretnick,' in a woman's voice.

I shook it, thinking one of the wires had come loose.

'Toller bandol venting,' said a man's voice.

'Charlie,' I whispered. 'Listen to this.'

He walked over and crouched down in time to hear the woman's voice say, 'Loy. Loy garting dendle. Nets?'

Our jaws dropped and our eyes widened.

'Zorner.'

'Zorner ment. Cruss mo plug.'

'Bo. Bo. Tractor bonting dross.'

'Are you hearing what I'm hearing?' asked Charlie.

'I am. But who is it?'

Charlie listened carefully. 'That's Mrs Pearce.'

'Wendo bill. Slap freedo gandy hump,' said Mrs Pearce.

'God, you're right. But who's the other one?' I turned the volume up and concentrated.

'Zecky?' said the man's voice. 'Spleeno ken mondermill.'

'It's Mr Kidd,' I said.

'I think my head is about to explode,' said Charlie.

'Wait . . .' I fiddled with every knob on the walkie-talkie. I took the batteries out and put them in again. There was no getting away from it. Our art teacher and our history teacher were standing in the empty staff room saying 'Tractor bonting dross' and 'Slap freedo gandy hump' to each other like it was the most natural thing in the world.

'Gasty pencil,' said Mrs Pearce.

'Spudvetch!' said Mr Kidd.

'Spudvetch!' Mrs Pearce repeated.

Two chairs scraped back, four shoes clicked across the floor, the door opened, the door closed and then there was silence.

Charlie and I looked at each other and raised our eyebrows in unison. We didn't say anything. We didn't need to. We were thinking the same thing.

Forget Fenham. There was an adventure on its way, a nuclear-powered, one-hundred-ton adventure with reclining seats and a snack trolley. And it was pulling into the station right now.

# 4

# doing it the simple way

**W**hen I got home I had plenty of time to think about what Charlie and I had heard, on account of being locked in the bathroom for an hour and a half.

I strode into the flat, threw my school bag into my bedroom and headed to the kitchen to grab a hot chocolate. Unfortunately, the kitchen was already occupied by my sister and Craterface.

'Howdy!' I chirruped.

My head was so full of Mr Kidd and Mrs Pearce and 'Tractor bonting dross' that I had completely forgotten about the flying sandwich and the death threat until Craterface lunged at me, shouting, 'Come here, you little snotrag!' – at which point it all came flooding back.

I squealed and leaped out of grabbing range. I sprinted into the hallway, skidded into the bathroom and turned round. I saw a hideous flash of sideburns and flying fists, then I slammed the door and locked it.

'Come out and be killed!' he shouted, battering the flimsy plywood.

I wasn't stupid. I picked up the bottle of bleach, took the top off, pointed the nozzle towards the door and waited. The hinges strained but didn't give way.

Moments later I heard Dad wander out of his bedroom and mutter, 'What's all this then?'

Craterface replied that he was going to kill me. Becky said he didn't mean it. And Craterface said he did mean it.

I waited for Dad to kick Craterface out of the flat or knock him unconscious with a blow to the head. But he just ummed and erred and said, 'I'm going to the shop. If you're not gone when I'm back, there'll be trouble.'

I was beginning to see what Dad meant when he said that he wasn't a real man any more.

When the flat door banged behind him, Craterface laughed, hammered on the bathroom door a bit more, got bored and returned to the kitchen. Keeping the bleach to hand, I sat down on the fluffy blue bathmat and did some thinking.

And what I thought was this . . . They weren't talking nonsense. They weren't the sort of people who talked nonsense. Ever. Mrs Pearce was eighty-five, or thereabouts, and Mr Kidd had no sense of humour. No. What they were saying sounded exactly like a real conversation. It was just that you couldn't understand a word of it.

So they were talking a foreign language. Perhaps they used to live in Burkina Faso or the Philippines. Perhaps they'd gone on holiday to Greenland or Vietnam. Perhaps they went to Mongolian evening classes together.

In which case, why did we never see them talking at any other time? I couldn't remember them exchanging a single word in all the years I'd been at the school.

And if they spoke a foreign language, why hadn't they told us? They were teachers. Teachers loved showing off. Only last week Mr Kidd had been reminding us yet again of how he once played cricket for Somerset under-nineteens. And Mrs Pearce liked nothing better than sitting down at the piano during assembly and adding extra twiddly bits to the hymn music that weren't meant to be there. If they could speak Mongolian, you could bet your bottom dollar they'd tell us about it.

They'd waited until everyone was out of the room. They had a secret. And it was a big one. A really big one. A secret they didn't want us to know about. A secret they didn't want any of the other teachers knowing about.

And we were going to find out what that secret was.

I waited for an hour and a half and Mum finally came home from work. I stood up and pressed my ear to the door.

'Where's Jimbo?' she asked Becky.

Once again, I heard Craterface explaining that he was going to kill me. A nanosecond after that I heard a loud crunch. I later found out that this was the sound of Craterface being hit on the side of the head by a briefcase with a combination lock.

He yelped in pain. 'Wotcha do that for?'

'Out!' barked Mum, so loudly that even I jumped. 'Get your greasy backside out of this flat now, or I'm calling the police.'

'Take it easy, missus,' grumbled Craterface.

'Keep your hair on, Mum,' whined Becky.

'And less of your lip,' snapped Mum.

The sound of heavy boots was followed by a loud slam. Then Mum rapped quietly on the bathroom door.

'You can come out now, Jimbo. That oaf is gone.'

I came out and shook Mum's hand. 'That was classy.'

At least there was one real man in the family.

After all the commotion it turned into a surprisingly pleasant evening. Dad spent so long in the shop, for fear of coming back and finding Craterface still in residence, that he'd done enough shopping for three weeks. Toilet rolls, J-cloths, washing-up liquid, scouring powder, the works.

So Mum was happy. And Dad was happy that Mum was happy. And I was happy that Mum and Dad were happy with each other. Plus, Becky was really unhappy, which always cheered me up. And anyway, she just stayed in her room, sulking, so we had a very nice time indeed.

After I'd washed up I decided to go to bed and plan tomorrow's investigations. I got my hot chocolate and walked up to Dad, who was sitting in front of the TV, watching *Police, Camera, Action!*

'Spudvetch!' I said, catching his eye.

He looked at me in a puzzled way for a few seconds. Then he grinned and said, 'Spudvetch!' and gave me the OK sign.

I grinned back and headed off down the hall.

Charlie and I were in complete agreement. We couldn't ask them straight out. We had to be subtle. They had a secret, and they weren't going to give it away to any Tom, Dick or Harry who wanted to share it.

However, there were plenty of other things we could get away with asking. And, since I'd lost the toss, it was me who got to ask first.

My target was Mr Kidd. We trailed him over the lunch hour and followed him into the school library, where we found him browsing the Arsenal supporters' website on one of the computers.

I grabbed a book on Spain from the shelves, opened it, put my head down and bumped into him. 'Sorry, sir,' I said, stepping backwards.

'That's all right,' he replied, rapidly swivelling the monitor ninety degrees.

'Sir . . . ?' I asked, trying to force his eyes off the page.

'What, John?'

'It's Jim, sir.' I took a deep breath. 'I was thinking of learning some Spanish.'

'Really?' he said, looking at me rather oddly, as if I had food all over my face or a dangling bogey.

'We're going on holiday there, sir. Do you speak Spanish?'

'No,' he said warily. 'Why are you asking me these questions?'

'I was wondering how quickly I could learn a foreign language. Just the basics, I mean. If I really tried.' I took a second deep breath. 'Do you speak any other languages, sir?'

'Languages aren't really my strong point,' he sighed. 'I'm a pictures bloke, really. Now they stick in my head. But languages . . . Well, it's in one ear and out the other. I tried learning a bit of French in Brittany last year, but I sounded like an idiot. And if I'm going to sound like an idiot I'd prefer to do it in my own language.'

Charlie's target was Mrs Pearce.

He got his first chance three days later when the subject of explorers came up. Scott losing the race to the North Pole and dying on the way, Livingstone trekking up the Zambezi River, Captain Cook sailing to Australia and eating biscuits with weevils in them.

'Have you ever explored anywhere, Mrs Pearce?'

It was Charlie's voice. I twisted round in my seat. There was a small, bandaged hand sticking up in the air.

'Of course not,' replied Mrs Pearce, smiling and shaking her head.

She was right. It was a pretty stupid question. With her tweed suit and her handbag, I couldn't imagine Mrs Pearce exploring anything more dangerous than the freezer cabinet in Sainsbury's.

'I mean, haven't you been anywhere exciting?' Charlie soldiered on. 'Like Africa or India or someplace?'

It all sounded a bit heavy-handed to me. Charlie had

never shown much interest in history before. But she was delighted by his question.

'I'm afraid not,' she said, taking off her glasses and polishing them with her handkerchief. 'I've never actually been abroad. I go to Scotland most summers, but I don't think that counts as exploring.'

I was waiting for Charlie at the school gates, wondering what on earth we did now. If they had a secret, they were covering their tracks extremely well. So well that I was beginning to wonder if the conversation we overheard was nothing more than a very vivid dream.

'Jimbo,' panted Charlie as he ran up to me. 'Sorry I'm late. Had to get the walkie-talkie out of the staff room.'

'And what story did you tell this time?'

'Got the headmistress to sign me off sport for a month. You know' – he held up his bandaged hand – 'told her it was doctor's orders.'

'So what happens when the headmistress talks to your mum at the next parents' evening?'

Charlie shook his head. 'She never gets a word in edgeways.'

'So,' I said, getting back to the important subject, 'what do we do now?'

'We should have recorded them,' said Charlie. 'If we could play the conversation back then maybe—' He stopped mid-sentence and looked back towards the school. 'I've had an idea.'

I turned and saw Mr Kidd walking across the playground towards us, juggling his briefcase in one hand and his car keys in the other.

'All this suspense is driving me up the wall,' said Charlie. 'Let's do this the simple way.'

'What do you mean?' I asked, feeling slightly panicky.

Charlie stepped out into Mr Kidd's path. He waited until Kidd came to a halt in front of him, then said, in a cheery voice, 'Spudvetch!'

Mr Kidd froze for a second. Then his briefcase slid out of his hand and fell to the ground. He didn't seem to notice. His jaw started to move up and down but he was obviously having trouble getting any words out.

I started to feel a bit ill.

# boom!

'But you're not—' said Mr Kidd. Then he stopped himself.

His fingers clenched and his back stiffened like an angry cat's. And then something happened to his eyes. If Charlie hadn't seen it too, I might have thought I was imagining it. But I wasn't imagining it. For the briefest of moments there was a fluorescent blue light flickering behind his pupils, just like the eyes on Charlie's robot piggy bank. Except that Mr Kidd wasn't a robot piggy bank. He was our art teacher.

I was about to turn and run when, as suddenly as it had begun, it was all over. His eyes returned to normal. Slowly and deliberately he put his right hand over his left wrist, as if calming himself down. He breathed deeply and said, 'You off home, boys?'

I tried to say, 'Yes,' but it came out as a strangled squeak.

Charlie was on his knees, refilling Mr Kidd's briefcase. He stood up and handed it back.

'Thank you.' Mr Kidd smiled. 'I'll see you tomorrow, then. Have a good evening, boys.'

We stood and watched him walk into the car park. He pressed his key fob and the indicator lights on his battered Fiat winked back with a little *boop-boop* noise.

'Crikey,' said Charlie.

A swarm of fizzy white lights started floating across my field of vision. The sky started to spin round, my knees went wobbly and I had to sit on the wall to stop myself fainting.

# 5

# burglary

I woke up in the middle of the night, thinking that Mr Kidd was standing over my bed holding a bread knife, grinning broadly and saying, 'Have a good evening. Have a good evening. Have a good evening,' as the fluorescent blue light flickered in his eyes.

I checked inside the wardrobe. I checked under the bed. I checked the balcony and the bathroom and behind the sofa. And I still couldn't get back to sleep. So I found a packet of garibaldi biscuits and watched *Star Wars* until everyone else started waking up. Then I went into my room and pressed my forehead against the radiator for five minutes.

I came out and told everyone I had a sore throat and diarrhoea and it was clearly a very bad idea for me to go to school. Obviously I couldn't stay at home for ever. But for the time being I felt a lot safer lying on the sofa under a rug watching *The Empire Strikes Back* and *Return of the Jedi*.

'You poorly, poorly thing,' sighed Becky, who could read me like a book. 'I think we ought to call an ambulance, don't you? Shall I ring for one now?'

'Mum?' I said. 'I think I've got a temperature. Here. Feel.'

But Mum was too busy, whirling round the flat putting lipstick on and grabbing presentation folders. 'Get Dad to feel it, darling,' she said, checking her hair in the glass front of the cooker. 'I'm late already.'

'I'm ringing the hospital now,' announced Becky, picking up the phone.

'Act your age and not your shoe size,' snapped Mum, taking the receiver from her, slamming it back down and scooting through the door in a cloud of perfume.

Dad wasn't much help either. 'School is important,' he said, lying on the sofa, wearing his pyjamas and watching breakfast TV. 'Every day counts. You need education. You need exam results.'

'But, Dad. Feel my head. Quickly.' My forehead was cooling off. The radiator was painful and I didn't fancy doing it a second time.

'You need qualifications,' he said, giving me his top-grade, serious-father look. 'Qualifications are what stop you ending up sitting on the sofa in your pyjamas watching breakfast television while everybody else goes off to work.'

'But . . .'

'Jimbo' – he pointed his toast at me – 'you can still walk. You can still talk. You're not coughing blood and none of your bones are broken. Go to school.'

I thought about telling him the truth. The walkie-talkie. Spleeno ken mondermill. The robot-piggy-bank eyes. But it sounded crazy. And the last thing I needed was a weekly session with the school psychologist.

I went to get dressed, then picked up my bags and slouched out of the front door to the lift.

As it happened, there was nothing to worry about. We weren't bundled into the back of a van. We weren't strangled in the toilets by men in black balaclavas. Mr Kidd nodded a polite hello to us in the corridor and Mrs Pearce did the Boer War without batting an eyelid.

By lunch time I had convinced myself that it was nothing. Mr Kidd wore strange contact lenses. Or we'd seen the blue light of a police car reflected in his eyes.

He and Mrs Pearce were members of an Esperanto club, or sharing some obscure joke. I didn't care what. I just wanted to forget the whole thing and stop being scared.

Of course, Charlie wasn't going to let that happen. 'Come on, Jimbo,' he said. 'This is hot stuff. Tell me the last time anything this exciting ever happened to either of us.'

The answer was 'never'. I didn't say it.

He soldiered on. 'Perhaps there's a boring explanation. Perhaps there isn't. Perhaps Kidd and Pearce are bank robbers talking in code. Perhaps they're drug dealers. Perhaps they're spies.'

I mumbled incoherently.

'I'm going to follow them,' said Charlie. 'I want to know what they do after school. I want to know where they go and who they speak to. Because they're up to something. I know it. And I'm going to find out what it is. So . . . are you in? Or not?'

'Charlie,' I said, 'I just need to get some sleep.'

'Suit yourself.'

# boom!

I got home to one of Dad's classic dinners. It was called shepherd's pie, apparently. Though it wasn't like any other shepherd's pie I'd ever tasted. I think Dad just arranged a pile of meat and potatoes in a large baking dish, then attacked it with a blowtorch. It looked like something pulled out of a house fire.

I took a mouthful, then gave up. Becky took a mouthful, then gave up. Mum told us to stop being so fussy. Then she took a mouthful, retched visibly and used a word that parents really shouldn't use in front of children. And we all had a double helping of pears and custard to make up for the lack of main course.

Craterface turned up at the door after supper but Mum told him that he wasn't allowed into the flat until he'd apologized to me. Apologizing was not really his thing so he and Becky departed in a monstrous huff. Mum then went off to do some paperwork in the bedroom and Dad and I sat down to watch *The Phantom Menace*. It felt good sitting next to Dad. It was like being little again. All in all I had pretty good parents, I reckoned. Dad might occasionally try to poison me, but he never attacked me with secateurs.

I fell asleep just after Darth Maul tries to assassinate Qui-Gon Jinn. Dad must then have carried me to the bedroom because the next thing I knew I was waking up after eight hours' quality sleep, feeling a good deal better.

Charlie was a bit stand-offish at school. I'd offended him by not wanting to be involved in Phase Two of the plan. But I'd made up my mind. I'd had enough stress over the last few days. I didn't want to be caught stalking a teacher. I told myself to be patient. Charlie would get bored soon. Or he'd be caught and hauled in front of the headmistress and given a string of detentions. Either way the result would be the same. Life would return to normal.

We met up at the gates after school, like we did most days, and I asked if he wanted to come round to the flat.

He didn't. 'Things to do. People to watch,' he said, patting his pocket mysteriously and heading off to the bus stop.

So I wandered into town on my own, went to Waterstone's and bought a copy of *500 Recipes for Beginners*. I splashed out on gift wrapping, then made my way home.

Dad didn't know whether to be deeply touched or

slightly offended. I told him I'd spent a large chunk of my pocket money, so he'd better use it. I didn't want my parents getting divorced. And if that meant Dad learning how to make a proper shepherd's pie, then he had to learn how to make a proper shepherd's pie.

'It's like building a model aircraft,' I said. 'You just follow the instructions.'

I was wrong about Charlie. He wasn't getting bored. And he hadn't been caught. Every time I bumped into him he said, 'Sorry, Jimbo. On a job. Can't stop.'

I was getting lonely. And bored. And irritated.

On Sunday morning, however, I was sitting on the wall of the park opposite the flats trying to remember what I used to do with myself before Charlie came along and wondering which of my non–best friends I should ring. Suddenly Charlie materialized next to me.

'God, you made me jump.'

Using his unbandaged hand he slid an orange notebook out of his pocket. The word *Spudvetch!* was written across the cover.

'What's this?'

'Open it,' said Charlie.

I opened it. It was Mr Kidd's diary. Except that it wasn't written by Mr Kidd. It was written by Charlie.

FRIDAY

6.30   Sainsbury's (sausages, bran flakes, shampoo, milk, broccoli, carrots and orange juice).

8.00   Arsenal v. Everton on TV.

10.00   Takes rubbish out.

'Hang on,' I said. 'How do you know what he's watching on TV?'

'He didn't shut the curtains,' said Charlie.

'Yeah, but—'

'I was standing in his garden,' said Charlie. 'There's a gap in the fence.'

'You're crazy.'

I returned to the book. There was a map. And there were photographs.

The second half of the notebook was devoted to Mrs Pearce. Diary. Map. Photographs. There was even a photocopy of her library card. It was the kind of notebook you find in a psychopath's bedside table. Next to the voodoo dolls and automatic weapons. I began to wonder whether Charlie was losing his mind.

'They live like monks,' he said. 'They don't go to the pub. They don't visit friends. They do their shopping. They weed the garden. They clean the car.' He looked at me. 'Don't you think that's suspicious?'

'No,' I said. 'Suspicious is when you have a bunker under the house, Charlie. Suspicious is when you leave home wearing a false beard. Suspicious is when you visit a deserted warehouse with a hundred thousand pounds in a suitcase.'

He wasn't listening. 'I'm going to have to get inside one of their houses. Mrs Pearce's probably. Better access. Thursday evening. During the teachers' meeting. I need to have a poke around.'

'No,' I said. 'No, no, no, no, no. Have you any idea what will happen if you get caught? The police. The headmistress. Your parents . . .'

It was a stupid, insane, suicidal idea. Which makes it quite hard to explain why I decided to help. I guess it boils down to this. Charlie was my best friend. I missed him. And I couldn't think of anything better to do. Really stupid reasons which were never going to impress the police, the headmistress or my parents.

Looking back, I reckon this was the moment when my whole life started to go pear-shaped.

On Thursday evening we jumped onto a number 45 bus, got off at Canning Road and went into the park at the bottom of Mrs Pearce's garden. Ideally we would have gone in after dark, but Mrs Pearce never left her house after dark so we had no choice.

We waited for a small group of boys to disappear from round the swings, then headed over to the fence. And it was only then that a really important question occurred to me.

'Charlie?'

'What?'

'How are we going to get in?'

He smiled and extracted a key from his pocket.

'You stole her house key?' I couldn't believe it.

'No, Jimbo,' said Charlie. 'I borrowed it. Last week. She puts it under the flowerpot when she goes out. I popped into town and got a copy made.'

I didn't know whether to be impressed or horrified. Still, I reasoned, if you were going to break into someone's house it was probably better to let yourself in through the door, rather than smashing a window.

'We don't have much time,' said Charlie. 'Let's go.'

boom!

Once we were inside I began to see what Charlie meant. The house wasn't just ordinary. It was super-ordinary. Creepy ordinary. Like a film set. Floral china. A tea tray. The *Radio Times*. A little silver carriage clock on the mantelpiece. A tartan shopping trolley by the front door. It really *did* look suspicious.

We opened drawers. We looked in cupboards. We looked under the sofa. Quite what we were looking for I had no idea. On the other hand, if we were acting logically we wouldn't have been in the house in the first place.

With every passing minute a cold hand was starting to close around my heart, and when the clock struck five I gripped Charlie's arm so hard I left nail-marks.

Upstairs was just as characterless as down. There was a travel guide to Scotland. But that was the only piece of evidence that a real, living, breathing human being lived here.

'Right,' I said. 'Let's get out.'

'We haven't done the loft,' said Charlie.

'Are you out of your tiny mind?' I whispered.

He was. On the other hand, I didn't want to leave the

house on my own. If I was going to bump into Mrs Pearce I wanted to do it with company.

Charlie climbed onto the banisters, lifted the square white hatch and moved it to one side.

'Please, Charlie,' I said. 'Don't do this.'

But Charlie wasn't taking advice. He grabbed the side of the hatch and hoisted himself up into the darkness. He vanished briefly, then his head reappeared. 'Now you. Climb onto the banisters.'

I climbed onto the banisters and he reached down and pulled me up. When I was inside the loft Charlie took a torch from his back pocket with his working hand and I followed the oval of light as it swept over the joists.

There was a box of Christmas decorations. There were some old floor tiles. There was an empty suitcase. There was a spider the size of a gerbil.

'There's nothing here,' I said. 'Please, Charlie. I want to go home now.'

But he was making his way over to the hot-water tank and the pile of elderly cardboard boxes sitting around it. One by one he started to open them and investigate the contents. I crouched next to him and started to help so we could get this over and done with as quickly as possible.

It was me who found it. A metal biscuit tin pushed into

the recess beneath the tank. I pulled it out, blew the dust off, held it in the beam of Charlie's torch and popped the lid open. Inside were seven brass wristbands, an Ordnance Survey map of somewhere in Scotland and a piece of paper. Except that it wasn't paper. At least, not any kind of paper I'd ever seen. It was like tin foil, but smoother and softer. Yet when I unfolded it I could feel that it was as strong as leather. On it was printed:

*Trezzit/Pearce/4300785*

*Fardal, rifco ba neddrit tonz bis pan-pan a donk bassoo dit venter. Pralio pralio doff nekterim gut vund Coruisk (NG 487196) bagnut leelo ren barnal ropper donk gastro ung dit.*

*Monta,*

*Bantid Vantresillion*

'We have hit the jackpot, baby,' said Charlie.

And that was the exact moment when we heard Mrs Pearce come in through the front door downstairs.

'Don't move,' said Charlie.

He stepped round me and slid the square panel back over the hatch, shutting us both into the attic, and for a

couple of seconds I thought I might be sick, which would not have been helpful.

'Charlie?' I whispered. 'What the hell are you doing?'

He tiptoed back round me and picked up the piece of stuff that wasn't quite paper.

'Charlie?'

'Shhh!'

He slipped the orange *Spudvetch!* notebook out of one pocket and a pen out of the other. Putting the torch in his mouth and holding the notebook open with the bandaged paw of his right hand, he began to copy the incomprehensible message.

I sat with my face in my hands and breathed deeply and counted slowly to calm myself down. It didn't work. Through the ceiling I could hear Mrs Pearce moving about, opening doors, rattling the cutlery drawer, filling the kettle. It occurred to me that we might very well be stuck in the loft until she left for school in the morning. And then it occurred to me that I would need to go to the toilet sometime between now and tomorrow morning. And then it occurred to me that I was going to be arrested for weeing through the bedroom ceiling of my history teacher.

'Done,' said Charlie, sliding the notebook back into his pocket and putting the message back into the biscuit tin. He pushed it under the water tank and repositioned the rest of the boxes. 'Now, let's make our getaway.'

'How, precisely, are we going to do that?' I asked.

He got to his feet, cracked his knuckles and said, 'Rev your engine, Jimbo.'

He put his hands against the roof, jiggled it and wiggled it, and after a minute or so a slate came free. He pushed his arm further through the hole and Frisbee'd the slate out into the night. There was a second's silence, then the slate hit a greenhouse with an almighty shattering of glass.

'Now,' said Charlie. 'Listen.'

We waited for the sound of the back door being opened, then Charlie said, 'Go, go, go.'

I lifted the hatch, slid it to one side and lowered myself onto the banisters. Charlie did the same and slotted the hatch back into place. We'd just begun to go downstairs when Mrs Pearce walked into the hallway below us. We froze. She hadn't seen us yet, but it was surely only a matter of seconds before she turned round.

She was standing very still, staring at the front door, watching something or listening for something. I felt a single drop of sweat make its way down my spine.

And then she did something we'd seen Mr Kidd do in the playground, just after his eyes went blue. Carefully, she placed her right hand over her left wrist and lifted her head for a few seconds. We couldn't see her face, we couldn't see her eyes, but something about the gesture gave me the willies.

Then it was over. Her arms dropped to her sides, she picked up her keys from beside the telephone, took her coat from the rack, opened the front door and stepped outside, shutting it behind her.

We sprinted down the stairs, along the corridor and through the kitchen. We unbolted the back door, ran across the garden and vaulted the fence before you could say, 'Barnal ropper donk.'

We didn't stop until we'd left the park and run for five or six streets. We finally came to a halt at a bus stop on the main road. I was petrified. I was out of breath. I looked at my hands and I could see them actually shaking.

'God,' said Charlie, 'that was fantastic.'

'Next time, Charlie,' I said, 'you're doing it on your own.'

I got home expecting a grilling. About where I'd been. And why I'd been there so long. And why I hadn't told anyone beforehand. But Mum was working late, Becky was out with Craterface and Dad was so engrossed in his cooking that he wouldn't have noticed me bringing a cow

# boom!

into the flat. I dumped my bag and sat down. He took a spoonful of something from the pan on the cooker and carried it carefully over to me. 'Try this.'

So I tried it. And it was really very good indeed.

'Tomato and orange soup,' said Dad, 'with basil and cream and a dash of cognac.'

'Wow,' I said. 'Mum definitely won't divorce you now.'

# 6

# captain chicken

Charlie's bandages came off a couple of days later. To celebrate the occasion his mum decided that I should be allowed back into the house. He'd suffered enough, apparently. And learned his lesson. Clearly she knew absolutely nothing about her son.

On the other hand, it did give us the opportunity to show the secret message to Charlie's dad. Obviously we didn't want him leafing through the *Spudvetch!* notebook and finding out that Charlie had been following teachers around Sainsbury's. So we made a second copy on a clean sheet of paper and handed it to him over supper.

'What do you make of this?' asked Charlie.

Charlie's dad was, in our opinion, the brainiest person we knew. So if anyone could help us translate the mystery language, it was him.

Dr Brooks cleaned his lips with the corner of his

napkin, ferreted in his pocket for his reading glasses, eased them behind his ears and squinted hard. 'A code. Gosh, how delightfully old-fashioned.' He smiled quietly to himself. 'I thought kids these days just went around shoplifting and playing computer games. Where did this come from?'

'Confidential,' said Charlie.

'My, my,' replied his dad, winking at us. 'What fun.'

'So . . . ?' pestered Charlie.

Dr Brooks shook his head. 'It's all Greek to me, I'm afraid.'

'Greek?' I said excitedly.

Charlie's dad looked over the rim of his glasses. 'It's a phrase, Jim. All Greek to me. Double Dutch. Nonsense. Gibberish.'

'Ah,' I said, blushing slightly.

'Mind you . . .' he continued, popping the last new potato into his mouth and chewing contentedly. 'Coruisk. Now that rings a bell. I mean, it may just be a coincidence, but I think I've heard that word somewhere before. Coruisk, Coruisk, Coruisk . . . Do I get some sort of prize for working this out? Bottle of whisky? Book token?'

'I think we could manage something along those lines,' replied Charlie.

But the conversation was interrupted by Dr Brooks's

bleeper. He took the little black thingamajig from his belt and examined it. 'That's the hospital, I'm afraid. No rest for the wicked.'

'See you later,' said Charlie.

'And I shall have a jolly good think about that word.' He smiled, standing and taking his jacket from the back of the chair. 'But right now I must go and have a poke around with a dead body.'

On my way out of the Brooks's house, Charlie's mum stopped me and told me to wait for a minute. I thought I was about to get a lecture about keeping her ill-behaved son on the straight and narrow, but she returned after a minute or so carrying a large, metal, fish-shaped object.

'I very nearly forgot,' she said. 'This is for your father. He rang earlier to ask whether he could borrow my salmon mousse mould. Now, Jim, I am sure your father is a very trustworthy chap, but will you try and make sure he actually cooks with this? I don't want it welded into a scaled-down Wellington fighter-bomber.'

'I will.'

# boom!

I got home to find Dad with his sleeves rolled up, wearing a stripy apron and cutting a large aubergine into thin circular slices.

'Stir those onions, will you, Jimbo?' He pointed to a pan on the stove.

I dropped my bag, took off my tie and dutifully whisked the onions round a bit.

'What happened to the planes, Dad?' I asked.

'Planes, Jimbo?' He started dipping the aubergine slices in little bowls of egg and flour. 'I can do planes. I can do helicopters. I can do radio control. I can do aileron wiring and stall cut-outs. I need a challenge. You've got to progress. Turn the gas on under the frying pan. Thanks. You've got to learn new things. Keep yourself sharp.'

'Stops you sitting on the sofa in your pyjamas watching breakfast television while everybody else goes off to work.'

'Indeed,' said Dad.

Mum thought the Aubergine Parmesan was delicious. I had to agree. Even Becky liked it. 'It's all right,' she said glumly, which is high praise from a teenage death metal fan.

Dad grinned stupidly all through supper as if he'd just won an Oscar. And Mum grinned back at him like she'd just met him for the first time and fallen madly in love. At one point they were holding hands at the table. All of which made me a bit queasy, though I guess I couldn't complain.

The only sour moment was when Becky went to the cupboard to fetch a bottle of ketchup. Dad told her ketchup was an insult to good food. For a moment I thought there might be actual fisticuffs, but she looked around the table, realized it was three against one and decided to accept defeat.

After dinner I escaped to the balcony in case Mum and Dad did actual kissing and I vomited. Becky joined me soon after and said, 'What's got into him?'

'Into who?' I asked.

'Into Dad, stupid,' she said, lighting a cigarette and

dropping the match down on Mrs Rudman's balcony. 'All this cordon bleu business.'

'I bought him a cookery book,' I said.

She gave me a funny look. 'So it's your fault.'

'I think it is,' I said proudly.

'God,' she sighed, 'it's like he's turning into a woman.'

I patted Becky on the back. 'Women going out to work. Men cooking. You've just got to face it, sister. This is the modern world.'

It felt very strange being taught by Mrs Pearce on Monday. I kept wondering if she knew we'd been inside her house, whether she'd found something out of place, whether we were under suspicion. But her behaviour was no different from usual. So I soon relaxed and started to feel rather smug. We'd got away with it. She might have a secret. But we had a bigger one. It was one of the very few times in my life that I knew something a teacher didn't.

Mr Kidd seemed less scary too. We were on to them.

He might have scared the living daylights out of us. But if he knew how close we were getting it would probably scare the living daylights out of him.

We thought we were absolutely brilliant.

And it wasn't until the following Saturday morning that we realized how wrong we were.

I got up early and helped Charlie with his paper round. When it was done we cycled over to the shopping centre for a late breakfast at Captain Chicken. I bought myself a strawberry milkshake and an apple pie. Charlie opted for turkey nuggets and a black coffee, which he thought was more sophisticated.

'Any developments?' I asked.

He took out the orange *Spudvetch!* notebook and opened it at the page where he'd copied out the mystery message.

'I've Googled everything,' he said. 'Fardal is a surname. Rifco make bathroom cabinets. Bassoo is the name of a creek in Montana. And Pralio sell sports equipment.' He took a sip of his black coffee. 'On the other hand, you can stick any combination of letters into Google and find something. But here's the interesting thing. Remember Dad saying Coruisk rang a bell?'

'Uh-huh.' I blew bubbles into my milkshake.

'Well—' said Charlie. Then he fell silent.

'What?' I asked.

He was looking over my shoulder. I turned round. A man in a very expensive light-grey suit was walking towards us from the counter carrying a paper cup, a napkin and a burger box. The place was pretty much empty at this time in the morning but he came and sat down on the spare seat at the end of our table.

He was fifty or sixty years old and ridiculously tall. His face was tanned and wrinkly, like he'd spent most of his life outdoors. And despite the suit there was something worryingly military about his cropped grey hair.

He adjusted his suit, opened the burger box, unfolded his napkin, took a sip of hot chocolate and began eating his chicken burger, carefully keeping his pressed white cuffs away from the onion relish.

'Excuse me,' said Charlie. 'We'd like some privacy. If you don't mind.'

He said nothing. He looked at Charlie. He looked at me. He finished his mouthful. He wiped his mouth with his napkin. 'You think you're pretty clever, don't you?'

It was a posh voice, the sort of voice that introduces classical music on Radio Three. He didn't sound like someone who usually ate his breakfast in Captain Chicken.

I said nothing. Charlie slid the *Spudvetch!* notebook back into his pocket. 'Sometimes we're clever,' he said. 'Sometimes we're stupid. It kind of depends.'

The man smiled and took another bite of burger. Charlie and I began shuffling our bums towards the aisle.

'I don't know exactly how much you know,' the man continued, washing the burger down with another sip of hot chocolate. 'You know a little. That much is quite clear.'

He was clearly not your average weirdo.

'The Watchers brought you to my attention a few days ago. We have had you under surveillance since then. They are of the opinion that you are not dangerous. I'm not so sure.'

*The Watchers? Surveillance? Dangerous?* I felt the building tilt slightly to one side. Or was it me? I held the sides of my seat for support.

'The Watchers get nervous.' He brushed the bun-crumbs off his silk tie. 'The Watchers do not enjoy people poking into their affairs. And if you carry on as you have been doing, then they may decide that action has to be taken.'

He let the word 'action' hang in the air.

# boom!

'Who are you?' asked Charlie.

I kicked him under the table. I wanted this conversation to end. And I wanted it to end now.

But Charlie took no notice. 'What right have you got to come in here and tell us what we can and can't do?'

I kicked Charlie for a second time.

And that's when I saw it again, for a fraction of a second. A fluorescent blue flicker inside the man's eyes. He smiled. 'Who I am is not important. Nor am I going to tell you. Only one thing is important and it is that you stop your little games.'

As he spoke these words he pulled back one of his cuffs and pressed the tip of his forefinger to the surface of the table. I pushed myself further back into my seat. The end of his finger began to glow with an eerie neon-blue light. And the plastic tabletop under his finger started to blister and melt.

'It's very simple,' he explained, beginning to move his hand along the table. 'You have a choice. You can behave. Or you can face the consequences.'

The air began to fill with black smoke and the stink of burning plastic. He was slicing the table in two, the heat from his glowing finger eating through the surface like a soldering iron.

When he'd finished, we could see his polished black

shoes through the gash down the centre of the table.

'Do you understand?'

I nodded.

'Yes,' said Charlie. 'We understand.'

And then the man did what we'd seen both Pearce and Kidd do. He put his right hand over his left wrist. It had always looked as if they were calming themselves down. Now I saw what they were really doing. Around his left wrist was a brass band, just like the ones we'd found in Mrs Pearce's attic. He pressed it briefly with the fingers of his right hand, then let it go.

'Good.' He stood up. 'In that case I shall bid you good day. Charles . . . James . . .'

And with that he was gone.

We sat there, stunned, for several seconds. Then Charlie looked down and said, 'This smells really, really bad,' and a spotty bloke in a Captain Chicken hat started walking towards us, saying, 'What the hell have you done to my table?'

We ran.

# boom!

Five minutes later we were sitting on a bench in the little park in front of the flats.

'Gordon Bennett!' said Charlie.

'Gordon Reginald Harvey Simpson Bennett Junior!' I replied.

We were silent for a few moments. Then Charlie said, 'You saw that thing he did with the wristband?'

'Yeah,' I said. 'Kidd did the same thing. So did Pearce.'

'I know.' He fished in his pocket, and suddenly there it was in Charlie's hand – a wristband.

'You nicked one?' I asked incredulously. 'From the box in the loft? Charlie, that is seriously not a good idea.'

'Bit late now,' said Charlie. 'She had a whole pile. I was kind of hoping she didn't count them very often.'

'Charlie, you idiot.' Horrible pictures filled my head. The most horrible one involved me being cut in half by a hot neon-blue finger. 'Get rid of it. Get rid of it now. If they find out . . .'

'OK,' said Charlie. 'Point taken. But first . . . a little experiment.'

He pressed the bangle. Nothing. He squeezed it. Nothing.

'That guy was not joking,' I insisted. 'Please, Charlie. Chuck it.'

Then he put it on his left wrist, placed his right hand over it and pressed it.

'Snakes on a plane!' hissed Charlie, pulling his hand away as if he'd just touched an electric cooker ring. 'Try it,' he said, taking it off and handing it to me.

'No way,' I said, holding up my hands. 'Absolutely not.'

'Just put it on,' he insisted, taking my arm. 'This is important.'

I struggled briefly, then gave up. Wincing, I tensed my muscles as Charlie slipped the thing over my wrist.

'Now touch it.'

'Is it painful?'

'No, it's not painful, you big girl's blouse.'

I touched it with the fingers of my right hand and a high-pitched scream roared through my head as if a plane were landing somewhere between my ears. This was followed by a few clicks. Then I heard a voice saying, 'Gretnoid?'

I spun round to see who was talking to me. But there was no one there. We were alone in the park, apart from Bernie, the homeless guy, asleep under the hedge in the corner.

'Adner gretnoid?' said the voice. 'Gretnoid? Parliog mandy? Venter ablong stot. Gretnoid?'

boom!

It was coming from inside my own head. It was like having earphones screwed directly into your brain. I took my hand away and tore off the band.

'Heavy, eh?' Charlie nodded.

I decided it was time to go home and lie down.

# 7

# raspberry pavlova

I got into the lift. An elderly lady stepped in behind me with two bags of shopping. Was she a Watcher? Was she going to stop the lift and attack me with a luminous finger? I bent my knees a little, trying to see whether she was wearing a brass wristband. She gave me a worried look and left the lift at high speed when it reached her floor.

Were Pearce and Kidd the Watchers? Were there more of them? And why were they watching?

I got out and sprinted down the corridor, found my key, fumbled it into the lock, ran inside and slammed the door behind me.

'Are you all right, Jimbo?' asked Mum, holding a little orange watering can.

'No,' I said. 'No. I'm not all right.'

'What's the problem?' She put the watering can down on the phone table.

I stared at her. What could I possibly say? I didn't want to end up talking to the police. I didn't want to end up talking to the headmistress. I didn't want to end up talking to a doctor.

Mum gave me a hug. 'Hey. You can tell me. You know that.'

I mumbled a bit.

'Have you done something bad?' she asked. 'Or has someone done something bad to you?' She was very good at this kind of thing.

'A tiny bit of the first thing,' I said. 'But mostly the second.'

'Well, tell me about the second thing. That's the important one.'

I mumbled again.

'Is someone bullying you?'

Yes, I thought, that was a pretty good description. I nodded.

'Do you want me to talk to one of your teachers?' asked Mum.

I shook my head.

She ruffled my hair. 'They do it because they're weak. You know that, don't you? Bullies are cowards at heart. They only feel safe when other people are frightened of them.' She took hold of my shoulders and looked down at me. 'And if you need me or Dad to come into school, just say the word, all right?'

'Thanks,' I replied.

'Hey, Jimbo,' said Dad, sticking his head out of the kitchen door. 'Come and help me decide on the menu for tomorrow night. I need something to follow the salmon mousse and the duck. It's going to be a spectacular, a real spectacular.'

I flicked through *500 Recipes for Beginners,* plumped for the raspberry pavlova, then went and knocked on Becky's bedroom door.

I had to talk to someone. I had to talk to someone immediately. And I had to talk to someone who wasn't going to blab to the headmistress or the police or the nearest mental hospital. Unfortunately the only available person in that category was my sister. She wasn't an ideal choice but I was at the end of my tether. If the only thing she said was, 'That's awful,' or 'Don't worry,' it might make me feel a little better.

'Yeah?' she said.

# boom!

I pushed the door open and stepped inside.

'Becky?' I said, sitting down on the bed. 'I've got to talk to you.'

'What about?' she asked grumpily, staring into the mirror and applying her black eyeliner.

'This is going to sound really stupid . . .'

'That's pretty much par for the course,' she said, finishing off her eyes and starting to backcomb her hair. 'So why don't you just get it over with?'

'I'm in trouble.'

'Going to chuck you out of school, are they?' she laughed.

'Shut up and listen,' I snapped.

Something in my voice persuaded her that I was serious. She put her comb down and turned to face me.

'I'm all ears, baby brother.'

'You know Mrs Pearce and Mr Kidd?'

'I've been at that school for eight years, Jimbo.'

'OK, OK,' I apologized. 'Well, they're . . .' I took a deep breath. 'They're out to get me and Charlie. They speak this strange language when no one is around. They've got these brass wristbands that send messages into their heads.' I was gabbling, but I couldn't stop myself. 'And they're called the Watchers. At least, I think they're called the Watchers. Although the

Watchers might be someone else. And we were spying on them. And this really weird guy sat down next to us in Captain Chicken. And he told us to stop spying on them. And his finger glowed and he sliced through the table with it . . .'

I ground to a halt. Becky was looking at me as if I had a tap-dancing hamster on the top of my head.

'Becky, Becky,' I stammered. 'I know it sounds unbelievable, but it's true. Really. Cross my heart.'

She stared at me for a few more seconds, then said slowly, 'I don't know what you're up to, Jim. I know I was having you on about getting expelled and all that. It was a joke, OK? And you deserved it. But I am not going to fall for this guff just so you can get your own back. Drop it, right? You're cross with me. Fine. I apologize. End of story.'

She picked up her lipstick and turned back to the mirror.

I didn't even try to sleep. I waited until everyone else had retired to bed. Then I crept out of my room, made myself a Cheddar cheese and strawberry jam sandwich, sat down in front of the TV and discovered that the DVD player was broken.

I watched the highlights of the World Chess Championship. I watched an Open University prog- ramme on diseases in pigs. I watched the first fifteen minutes of a scratchy black and white film called *Son of Dracula*. But I had to switch off the TV when he crawled down a castle wall and turned into a bat. I turned on the radio. I played four games of patience. I played myself at Scrabble. I did the easy crossword in the paper.

At seven-thirty in the morning Dad sauntered into the kitchen in his dressing gown, did a double take and said, 'Goodness me, Jimbo, you're up bright and early for a change. Full of the joys of life, eh? Can't wait to get started on the day?'

And with that he began to rustle up a breakfast of fresh coffee, grapefruit slices, croissants, blueberry conserve and wild mushroom omelette.

Only when Mum and Becky had both emerged from their bedrooms did I finally feel safe enough to sleep. I went through to the living room, lay down on the sofa and passed into a coma.

Mum woke me seven hours later, saying that Charlie was on the phone wanting to speak to me urgently.

I sat up and waited for a few seconds until I could remember who I was and where I was and what day it was. I got to my feet and stumbled out to the hall.

'Jimbo?' he said.

'Nnnn . . .' I grunted. 'Charlie?'

'Yeah, yeah, it's me. Listen . . .'

'Yep.'

'I need you over here, asap.'

'What's the time?' I asked.

'Half five. Get your skates on. Dad solved the puzzle. You remember? Coruisk?'

'So what does it mean?'

'I'll tell you when you get here,' said Charlie.

I looked up. Mum was standing further down the hall, wagging her finger at me. Behind her Dad was slaving over a hot stove.

'Sorry, Charlie,' I said. 'Just remembered. It's Dad's big meal tonight. His spectacular.'

'Jimbo,' he insisted, 'this is important.'

'I know, I know,' I apologized. 'But this meal means a lot to him. Can't it wait?'

'Jeez, Jimbo, I thought we were . . .' He trailed off. 'OK. School. Tomorrow. We'll talk then.'

'Course.'

The phone clicked off.

Dinner started with salmon mousse on a bed of green salad with home-made oatcakes. This was followed by duck à l'orange with roast potatoes and honey-glazed carrots. For dessert we had the raspberry pavlova I'd suggested. The food was fantastically good. And because Dad was in such an exceptionally good mood he let me have a glass of wine. For an hour or so I managed to persuade myself that the encounter in Captain Chicken was a figment of my imagination. I didn't think about Mrs Pearce or Mr Kidd. I didn't think about attics or burned plastic. I was with my family. And I loved my family. Except Becky. I hated Becky. But hating your sister was normal.

*raspberry pavlova*

I felt ordinary and safe. And thanks to all these things I went to bed at ten and slept like a log.

# 8

# goodbye, charlie

Charlie wasn't at school. I'd taken an early bus and waited at the gates. Eight hundred pupils walked past me. But no Charlie. I stayed put till the bell went, then loped up to the main doors.

Perhaps he was ill. Perhaps he was pretending to be ill because he had some cunning plan to work on at home. There was obviously a rational explanation. I just didn't know what it was yet.

Then the headmistress made an announcement during assembly and I knew that things were taking a serious turn for the worse.

After she'd told us about arrangements for the forthcoming sports day, Mrs Gupta tapped her on the shoulder and whispered something into her ear.

'Oh yes,' said the headmistress, 'I nearly forgot to mention. Mrs Pearce and Mr Kidd are both off sick. Their classes will be taken by two very nice supply teachers, Mr

Garrett and Miss Keynes.' She nodded towards the two new faces squeezed in at the end of the line of staff.

Something was badly wrong. It was too much of a coincidence. I tried to persuade myself that Charlie and his dad had solved the puzzle, that they'd gone to the police and that Mr Kidd and Mrs Pearce were already behind bars or heading for the nearest airport. But it didn't seem very likely.

I couldn't concentrate. I got a detention from Mr Kosinsky and another one from Mr Garrett and I simply didn't care.

After lunch I faked a migraine and went to the sick bay. I was given two paracetamol and a mug of tea and groaned dramatically until they rang Dad and told him to come and pick me up.

I carried on groaning dramatically all the way home on the bus. When we reached the doors to the flats, however, I apologized to Dad, told him I'd explain everything later, ran to the bike sheds, undid my lock and broke some kind of land-speed record getting to Charlie's house.

I went through their gate, hit the brakes, turned sideways and sprayed gravel all over Dr Brooks's car. I dropped the bike, ran to the door and pressed the bell.

After a few seconds Mrs Brooks loomed up behind the frosted glass and the door swung open. She lunged towards me, shouting, 'Where the hell have you been, you stupid, selfish, thoughtless little—' Then she stopped. 'Oh, it's you.'

Two hands appeared around Mrs Brooks's shoulders and moved her gently to one side as if she were an unexploded bomb. The hands belonged to Dr Brooks.

'Jim,' he said, his face blank, 'come inside and close the door.'

I stepped onto the mat and squeezed myself round Mrs Brooks, who was starting to cry. Dr Brooks chivvied me down the hall and into the living room.

'Where's Charlie?' I asked.

'Charlie's disappeared,' he said.

'What?' I tried to sound surprised.

'He went to bed last night. Usual time. He seemed, well, like he always does. But this morning . . . he simply wasn't there.' He shook his head slowly. 'We've got no idea where he's gone.'

Out in the hall, I could hear Charlie's mum wailing horribly.

'Look. You know Charlie. He gets into scrapes. He plays silly games. Do you have any idea where he might have gone?'

I took a deep breath. I was going to sound crazy. I was going to be in trouble. But now wasn't the time to be worrying about that. 'Charlie rang me last night,' I said. 'He told me to come over. He had something important to tell me. I couldn't come because Dad was cooking a big meal. It was about that code. Do you remember? Charlie said you'd solved the puzzle.'

'Yes,' said Dr Brooks. 'Yes, we did. Sort of. But I thought that was just a game. Are you saying it has something to do with—?'

'What was the answer to the puzzle?' I asked. 'He said you knew what Coruisk meant.'

He rubbed his face with his hands. 'Coruisk. It's a loch in Scotland. On the Isle of Skye. The numbers after it – the ones in brackets – they're a grid reference. You know, so you can find the place on an Ordnance Survey map.' He paused. 'You're not seriously trying to tell me that he's gone to Scotland?'

'Wait,' I said, holding my head. It was all falling into place. Mrs Pearce went on holiday to Scotland. She owned a book on Scottish castles. The map in the box of wristbands under the water tank – it was a map of Skye.

'Jim?' asked Dr Brooks.

'This is going to sound insane.'

'Go on,' he urged me.

'The code . . .'

'Yes?'

'It was someone's secret. They didn't want anyone to know about it.'

# boom!

'Who, Jim? Who?'

'Mrs Pearce. Mr Kidd. The history teacher. The art teacher. They were up to something.'

'Jim, what the hell are you talking about?'

'I'm being serious. And they weren't in school today.'

The doorbell rang.

'I'll be back,' said Dr Brooks. 'That will be the police.' He disappeared into the hallway.

They'd taken Charlie, I knew it. He'd used the wristband. The voice on the other end . . . They knew. He hadn't behaved. He was facing the consequences.

I had to find him. And to find him I needed clues. I needed the notebook. And I couldn't trust anyone. I skidded into the hallway and ran up the stairs. I reached Charlie's room. I pulled out drawers. I yanked up the loose floorboard. I looked in the wardrobe.

I found them under the mattress. The orange *Spudvetch!* notebook and the brass wristband. I shoved them into my pocket.

I stood up and saw the robot piggy bank on the windowsill. I emptied the contents into my hand. Eight pounds sixty-five. I shoved it into my other pocket.

When I came back downstairs I saw Dr Brooks standing in the middle of the hallway talking to a large ginger-haired policeman.

The policeman looked up at me. 'The doctor tells me you're a friend of Charlie's.'

'Yes,' I said.

'Well, perhaps you can help us,' he said, taking a small flip-top notepad out of his jacket pocket.

'Tell him what you told me,' said Dr Brooks. 'That stuff about Mrs Pearce and whatsisname – the art teacher.'

The policeman's eyebrows lifted. He stared at Dr Brooks. Then he stared at me. 'That sounds interesting,' he said.

'Well,' I began, steeling myself to tell the crazy story all over again.

'I know what' – the policeman smiled – 'why don't I give you a lift home? You can tell me all about it on the way.'

Dr Brooks nodded to me and said, 'It's OK, Jim, you go with Inspector Hepplewhite. We'll be all right here. Just ring and let us know if you remember anything.'

I was about to say that I had my bike in the drive when Inspector Hepplewhite reached out towards the door-knob. A moment sooner, a moment later and I wouldn't have seen it. His cuff lifted slightly and there it was. Round his left wrist. A brass band.

'No,' I said, taking a step back up the stairs. 'Thanks. But I'll be fine.'

'We've got some important things to talk about.' The

inspector began to chuckle in a way that was not very convincing. 'And I'm going to be late for my tea in the canteen. Come on. I can drop you off in a jiffy.'

I looked towards Dr Brooks for help, but he didn't know I needed help.

'I'd rather not,' I stammered.

The inspector walked over to me and I felt his hand around my arm. 'If you know things that are significant, you should tell us. Withholding information is a very serious offence.'

I began to pull away, but his grip was like an anaconda's. And all the time he was smiling a big, friendly policeman smile from the middle of his orange beard. If I didn't think fast, I'd be in that car. Once I was in the car, he'd find the wristband and the notebook and the message. And I'd disappear, like Charlie. There would be no one to look for me. And there would be no clues left except the name of a Scottish loch.

'Fine,' I said. 'I just need to go to the toilet first.'

'I'll wait for you here,' said the inspector.

I walked into the kitchen. There was no back door. I climbed onto the sink and opened the window. I was stepping across the draining board when I kicked over a large casserole dish. I tried to grab it but I was too late. It hit the stone floor with a sound like a gong being struck.

Suddenly the inspector was at the door, yelling, 'Hey! Get back in here!'

'Jim!' shouted Dr Brooks, in close pursuit. 'What are you doing?'

I launched myself through the window to the sound of china shattering behind me. I hit the grass and rolled over, with knives, forks and spoons raining all over me.

I got up, sprinted round the corner of the house, mounted my bike, executed a neat skid round the inspector as he burst out of the front door, rode back over the lawn, then careered through the wooden gate into the park and off through the trees.

I sprinted up the steps of the library, leaving my bike unlocked. I leaped through the doors and aimed myself at the information desk. I was breathing so hard I couldn't speak properly. 'Isle of Skye. Ordnance Survey map. I need the Ordnance Survey map. Isle of Skye. In Scotland.'

'Thank you, I do know where the Isle of Skye is.' With agonizing slowness the librarian extracted a grimy white handkerchief from her pocket and blew her nose.

Then she repocketed the handkerchief. 'If you'd like to follow me.'

Eventually we found ourselves in the map section. She led me to a shelf of pink spines. 'Typical,' she tutted. 'Everyone's always taking them out and putting them back in the wrong order.'

I pulled a random map out and turned it over. On the rear was a diagram of the entire country divided into little squares. The Isle of Skye was covered by maps 23 and 32. I ran my finger along the pink spines.

The librarian found 32. I found 23.

'Can I take them out?' I asked, extracting map 32 from her hands.

'I'm sorry,' she said, 'maps can't be borrowed. You'll have to read them here.'

It was not a day for worrying about fiddling details like library rules. I said, 'My name is Barry Griffin. I go to St Thomas's,' and sprinted for the exit.

Only when I reached the flats did I realize what a stupid idea it was, going home. Inspector Hepplewhite knew my address. And if he didn't, Charlie's father would tell him.

I overshot the car park, coming to a halt behind the garages. I got off my bike and poked my head round the corner. The car park was empty. The inspector had been and gone. Or hadn't got here yet. Or simply assumed I wasn't stupid enough to come back. My head reeled. If I was going to find Charlie, there was stuff I needed upstairs. I could be in and out in three minutes.

I decided to go for it. I ran across the vacant car park, banged through the swing doors and threw myself into the lift.

I let myself into the flat and shut the door firmly behind me.

I went into my bedroom. I emptied my own savings of nineteen pounds fifty-two from the cigar box and added them to Charlie's money. I pulled the old tent and one of the sleeping bags down from the hall cupboard and stuffed them into my big sports holdall. I grabbed a change of clothes and went into the kitchen and started filling a Sainsbury's bag with food: a loaf, a packet of biscuits, some of Dad's leftovers and a box of

boom!

Quality Street. I opened the wotsit drawer and took out a penknife, the first-aid kit, a torch and a roll of string. I went back into my bedroom and found a compass.

As I was doing this, the brass wristband fell out of my pocket. I picked it up and looked at it. Was this how they'd found Charlie? Was it sending out some kind of homing signal? I had to get rid of it. Except that I couldn't get rid of it. It was my one piece of proof, the one object I possessed which showed that I was not a deranged lunatic.

And then I remembered. Dad lost a plane last year. The park people put corrugated iron round the bandstand. The plane flew behind it, the radio contact cut out and it crashed into the boating lake. Radio signals couldn't travel through metal. He proved it by putting the radio in the oven and making it go silent.

I grabbed the roll of cooking foil from under the sink, tore off a large square and wrapped the wristband in several layers before shoving it back in my pocket.

Only when I had finished did I stop and stand still and listen to the ticking of the clock and the buzzing of the refrigerator and realize that the flat was completely empty. No Dad. No Becky. Where were they?

I suddenly felt cold all over.

# 9

# vroom

I took a deep breath. They were late, that was all. Mum was still at work. Becky was still at school. Dad would be . . .

Where would Dad be? I'd done a runner. He'd ring the school. He'd ring Charlie's parents. He might be round there right now. He might be talking to Inspector Hepplewhite. He might be locked up in a cellar some-where.

I rang his mobile. Nothing. I crossed the lounge, opened the glass door, stepped outside and looked over the balcony. Maybe he was on his way back here right now. But the car park was empty.

The glass door slid open behind me. I spun round. 'Dad?'

It was the man from Captain Chicken. The same suit. The same cropped grey hair. The same wristband under the same white cuffs.

# boom!

'I'm sorry, James,' he said smoothly. 'You know too much.'

'Where are Becky and Dad?' I said, backing up against the railings, my voice suddenly hoarse. 'What have you done with them?'

'Your father is at the police station. You ran away from Inspector Hepplewhite, remember? But I'm afraid the police won't have any idea where you are.' He shook his head sadly. 'Your sister is with that poorly-washed boyfriend of hers.'

'You . . . you . . . you . . .' I felt very small and very alone and very frightened.

'Goodbye, James. Unfortunately this is the bit where you die.'

I shoved him hard in the chest so that he staggered backwards, then I turned and grabbed the railing. Maybe I could climb over and swing down onto Mrs Rudman's balcony. I threw my leg over.

'James, James, James . . .' he sighed, clutching my arm and dragging me back onto the balcony. 'Don't waste your energy. You see the red Volvo?'

I looked down. A red Volvo was parked by the entrance to the flats. A man in a very expensive light-grey suit was leaning against the bonnet. A second man in a very expensive light-grey suit was standing nearby, idly kicking bits of gravel.

'Even if you got away,' he said, 'you wouldn't make it to the bottom of the stairs.'

My body went limp. There didn't seem to be any point in struggling.

Then I heard a familiar noise. It was still several streets away, but I would have recognized it anywhere. Craterface had taken the silencer off. It sounded like a Chieftain tank being driven at sixty miles an hour. The Moto Guzzi.

'I think we should do this inside,' the man said, tightening his grip and pulling me back towards the door. 'Where no one can see.'

I reached out and grabbed the railing again. If I could hold on for a few minutes until Becky and Craterface got up the stairs. If I could just—

'You're starting to really annoy me now,' he said, prising my fingers off the railing and shoving me through the sliding door into the lounge. The blue light had reappeared in his eyes and it was flickering like crazy.

I grabbed the curtains. They came off the rail. I grabbed an armchair, which turned over. I grabbed the sideboard and we were momentarily covered in a shower of biros and radio-controlled aircraft parts and Mum's decorative plates from Crete and Majorca. As I was manhandled through the hall, I swiped the paper knife from the phone table, twisted round and stuck it into the man's leg.

# boom!

He said nothing. He didn't shout. He didn't wince. He merely removed the paper knife, stopped in his tracks, held me against the wall with one hand and twisted the other into a crab-shape several inches from my face. Five hot neon-blue lights appeared on the ends of his fingers and thumb.

And that was when the front door opened. Becky stepped inside, saw me pinned to the wall and screamed like a cat having its tail screwed into a vice.

'What's up?' asked Craterface, coming in behind her.

The four of us stood looking at one another for several seconds, no one knowing quite what was meant to happen next.

Then the man raised his glowing hand towards Craterface. 'You. Back off.'

'Do something!' Becky shouted.

It was all the encouragement Craterface needed. He swept the greasy hair out of his eyes, inflated his chest and said, 'No one tells me to back off, mate.' He flattened his hands, kung-fu style, then leaped forward, roaring, like someone preparing to cut an aeroplane into slices.

The man in the suit let go of me so that he had two hands free to defend himself. Craterface was really very good at the kung-fu thing. He chopped the man in the side of the neck and he tumbled backwards through the kitchen door, fell over and got himself tangled in the ironing board. It was, I think, the first time I had ever seen Craterface looking genuinely happy.

Becky grabbed me by the collar and shouted, 'What the hell is going on, Jimbo?'

'Get me out of here!' I panted. 'Just get me out of here!'

'Wait!' she snapped. 'I need an explanation.'

She didn't get one. What she got were two neon-blue hands on her shoulders. One of the Volvo men had come upstairs to find out what the delay was. There were little blue fireworks in his eyes.

'Oi!' yelled Becky, spinning round.

There were two smoking hand-prints on her jacket and a smell of burned leather in the air.

'My jacket!' she shrieked. 'Look what you've done to my jacket!'

The motorcycle helmet, which had been dangling in her hand, executed a neat curve up over her shoulder and onto the head of the new arrival, who went cross-eyed, tottered a bit, then fell into a heap.

Becky turned to me. 'OK, Jimbo, you win,' she said quickly. 'You can explain later. Let's get out of this place.'

'Thanks,' I said, grabbing the second sleeping bag from the hall cupboard.

# boom!

Becky looked at the bag. 'Where are we going? Outer Mongolia?'

'Maybe,' I said.

I looked round and saw the fridge topple over onto the floor with an almighty crash.

'Terry!' shouted Becky. 'Are you all right?'

His ugly face appeared round the door. 'Course I am!' And he dived back into the fray.

Becky picked up Craterface's helmet, threw it to me and said, 'Take this.'

I grabbed his jacket too, for good measure.

All the way down the stairs Becky kept saying, 'This is totally insane. This is totally insane.'

'I know,' I said. 'I know. Please. Just keep moving.'

We ran across the car park and I began stuffing my supplies into the panniers of the Moto Guzzi. Only when I was locking them did I remember the second man in the very expensive light-grey suit, who was now running towards us.

'Becky!' I shouted. 'Watch out!'

She spun round. 'God, Jimbo, you have some really charming friends.'

She hopped onto the bike. I hopped onto the bike. Our pursuer realized he was going to need transport too, and he turned and ran back to the red Volvo. We buckled our helmets on.

'Have you ever driven this bike before?' I shouted.

'Of course not. Terry wouldn't let anyone else near it.'

'Oh my God.'

'There's always a first time!' she shouted.

The Volvo started up, screeched into reverse, then came at us like a fighter jet, with smoke pouring off its back wheels.

'Hang on!' shouted Becky.

I looked up at the flat and saw a kitchen chair fly out of a window. Then my head was yanked backwards, my bum was yanked forward and we were off.

Considering she was a learner driver, Becky did very well. Considering she was a learner driver being chased by an angry man in a large red Volvo, she was brilliant.

We lurched and roared and skidded. We mounted a pavement and came very close to hitting an ice-cream van. I turned and saw the Volvo lurching, roaring and skidding on our tail. We ski-jumped over a grassy mound and were airborne for a worryingly long time. We hit the ground, banked round a bus shelter and found ourselves on the main road.

So did the Volvo. As we accelerated down the dual carriageway, past the waterworks and the milk depot, I glanced round once more and saw the car only metres from our number plate.

'Faster, Becky!' I shouted. 'He's catching up.'

# boom!

I don't know whether she heard me. I don't even know whether she meant to do something quite so dangerous. Either way, without warning, I felt the bike swerve to the right, cut across the path of a large articulated lorry coming up behind us, leave the road and plunge through the shrubbery on the central reservation.

I closed my eyes. Branches clattered across the front of my visor and the bike bucked beneath us like a wild horse. I concentrated on keeping my lunch firmly down. I did not want to be sick inside a motorcycle helmet.

Then, suddenly, there was tarmac under the bike again. I opened my eyes and saw that we were travelling down the dual carriageway in the other direction. Twisting in my seat, I caught one brief and final glimpse of the red Volvo in the middle of the central reservation, its bonnet folded neatly round a tree trunk. Sticking out of the smashed windscreen was a sign reading: NO U-TURNS.

I told Becky she could slow down.

Ten minutes later we pulled up outside Tesco. Becky got off the bike, handed me the keys and said, 'Wait here. I'll be five minutes.'

'But, Becky . . .' I complained.

'Listen, mate,' she said, wagging her finger at me. 'If I'm going to Outer Mongolia, I need a toothbrush, I need eyeliner and I need some clean knickers.'

# 10

# the road north

Toothbrush, knickers and eyeliner on board, we roared away into the evening traffic. I directed Becky towards the motorway and after half an hour we pulled into a service station so that we could grab something to eat, fill up with petrol and have a team talk.

We bought ourselves a tray of scrambled eggs and chips and sticky cakes and made our way to a window seat. We squeezed in, Becky speared a chip, I took a sip of my lemonade and she said, 'Explanation. Now.'

I started at the beginning. The expulsion wind-up, bugging the staff room, Pearce and Kidd's mystery language, Charlie saying, 'Spudvetch!' to Mr Kidd, the raid on Mrs Pearce's attic . . .

Becky's chip remained suspended on the prongs of her fork, halfway between her plate and her mouth, throughout my entire story.

'Holy bananas,' she said. 'And this is all true?'

'Of course it is. You saw those men in the flat. They weren't pretending, were they?'

She let out a long, slow, whistly breath, then finally ate the chip.

'Look . . .' I said, reaching deep into a pannier. I took out the wristband and unwrapped the silver foil round it. 'Put this round your wrist.'

'So this is the thing?'

'Yeah, this is the thing,' I said. 'Now touch it with the fingers of your other hand. But be quick.'

She touched the brass bangle and jumped as the plane came in to land between her ears. 'What the flaming . . . ?'

Then the voice started. She whipped round, just like I'd done, thinking someone was standing next to her, talking into her ear.

I snatched the band off her wrist, wrapped it in the silver foil and slipped it back into the pannier.

'OK, OK, OK,' said Becky. 'I believe you. God, that totally freaked me out.'

I took another swig of lemonade. 'And I think it's got a kind of tracer on it, so we can't hang around here too long.'

She started eating her scrambled egg. 'Where are we going?'

'Loch Coruisk,' I said, burrowing in the pannier

again and bringing out the Ordnance Survey maps.

'Lock what?' asked Becky.

'Loch Coruisk,' I said. 'It's on the Isle of Skye.' I flattened out map number 32 across the table.

'Why there?'

'There was a message in the biscuit tin in Mrs Pearce's attic. It was in the same language they were using in the staff room. It said "Coruisk". Look . . .' I pointed to a jagged smear of blue in the centre of the map.

'And there was a map reference.' I dug out the *Spudvetch!* notebook and read out the numbers: 'Four-eight-seven-one-nine-six.' I followed the lines down from the top margin and the lines in from the left-hand margin. 'Here.' Where the lines converged there was a tiny square, indicating some kind of building by the mouth of the loch, where it fed into the sea.

'Yes,' said Becky, more insistently this time. 'But why are we going there?'

I looked up. 'I need to find Charlie. And it's the only clue we've got. The only one I can understand, anyway.'

Becky seemed unconvinced.

'This message – it was hidden under the water tank. In the attic. She really didn't want anyone to find it. It has to be important.'

I looked at the map again. It was like something from *The Lord of the Rings*. The loch was surrounded by the

Cuillin Hills. The peak of Druim nan Ramh to the north. The peak of Sgurr Dubh Mor to the south. It was eight miles from the nearest village. It was hard to imagine a more isolated spot.

'Do you realize how far away this place is?' asked Becky.

I crossed my fingers. I needed her. And I needed the Moto Guzzi. 'He's my best friend. And he's been kidnapped.'

'Maybe we should leave this to the police,' said Becky.

'Oh, yes, that's another thing.'

'What?' asked Becky.

'There was a policeman at Charlie's house.'

'And . . . ?'

'He was wearing one of the wristbands. He wanted me to get into his car. I ran away and he went berserk.'

'So the police are after you as well?' said Becky.

'Actually, they're probably after both of us now.'

'Brilliant,' said Becky. 'I'm travelling to the Isle of Skye with my baby brother on a stolen motorbike, without a driving licence, looking for someone who could be in Portugal for all we know. A secret society of mystery maniacs is trying to kill us. The police want to arrest us . . .'

Then I had a stroke of luck. I'd been fiddling with the

boom!

studs and tassels on Craterface's jacket when I noticed a large lump in one of the pockets. I stuck my hand inside and extracted a spanner, a packet of cigarettes, a cigarette lighter, a great deal of oily fluff . . . and a wallet.

Becky snatched it out of my hands, saying, 'Oi. You little thief.' But as she took it, the wallet popped open and a wad of ten-pound notes spilled across the map.

'What did he do?' I asked. 'Rob a post office?'

Becky was lost for words. Not something I'd seen very often.

'Ugly, but rich,' I said, knowing I was probably pushing my luck a bit too far.

She wasn't listening. She was counting the money. 'Two hundred. Three hundred.' She still had a long way to go. 'The lying pig,' she snapped. 'He told me he was broke. The stinking, two-faced, good-for-nothing, evil, self-centred . . .'

I let her rant for a bit. She needed to get this stuff off her chest. And I quite enjoyed it too. After a couple of minutes she ran out of steam.

I picked up a handful of tenners. 'This lot will get us to the Isle of Skye, won't it?'

Becky looked at me in silence for a few seconds, then hissed, 'Too damn right it will. If that creep thinks I'm hurrying home to see him, he's got another think coming. Let's hit the road, Jimbo.'

On our way out of the service station we remembered that we still had parents, and they were probably not too happy at the moment. So Becky called them on her mobile. Thankfully the answerphone was on.

'Mum. Dad. It's Becky. I've got Jimbo with me. We're both fine. But we can't come home right now. We'll explain everything later. Ciao.'

We filled the tank, bought two pairs of dark glasses and rejoined the motorway.

Night fell and Skye was still three hundred miles away. We turned off the M6 and wove our way down a maze of narrow country lanes until we came to a small wood. We parked the bike out of view of the road, clambered through the bushes and found ourselves a good tent-sized clearing.

There was a message from home on Becky's mobile, but we decided not to listen to it. After all, Mum and Dad weren't going to be wishing us luck.

The food I'd packed was cold and a bit battered,

but the remains of Dad's roast potatoes and raspberry pavlova were still good.

'Know what?' said Becky, brushing the crumbs from her lipstick.

'What?'

'I take back what I said about Dad.' She smiled. 'I don't care if he has got something wrong with his hormones. He produces some quality leftovers.'

We woke at dawn to find torrential rain had hammered its way through the canvas. The bottoms of our sleeping bags were soaked in grimy water. The shoes we'd put outside the mouth of the tent had all but dissolved.

'Why couldn't this have happened in July?' moaned Becky.

I wrung out the sleeping bags while she readjusted her make-up. Once her face was ready we squelched the tent down, squelched our belongings into the motor-bike panniers, squelched onto the damp leather seat and made our way back to the M6. Watching the glistening tarmac scoot by beneath my feet, I dreamed of duvets and hot breakfasts, big jumpers and radiators.

We had double beans on toast in Carlisle and spent a long time in the loos drying bits of clothing under the hand dryers. By Glasgow the sun had come out. By Dumbarton I was starting to feel almost human.

The countryside was looking stranger now, older, craggier. We twisted and turned along the banks of Loch Lomond for twenty miles. To our left mist hung between the peaks of high hills. To our right was mile after mile of water, all rippled in the wind and dotted with knobbly little islands with scrubby trees on them.

The road climbed. Crianlarich, Tyndrum, Ballachulish. The hills were barer now. In the sun it looked like a picture postcard. In the rain it would have looked like a scene from a horror movie.

My bum was beginning to hurt. We'd been driving for almost six hours now. So I was relieved when the hills started to fall away and we began making our way down towards the sea, to the Kyle of Lochalsh, and the Skye Bridge.

# boom!

We pulled off the main road and parked in front of a café by the water's edge. It was a popular place. Families were eating picnics on benches. Little kids were playing tag along the quay. Dogs were being taken out of the back of cars so they could pee on the verge.

We clambered off the bike, stretched our aching legs, then went and bought ourselves a couple of ice creams. Gulls wheeled overhead. A fishing boat chugged past.

'Cheers!' said Becky, knocking her cone against mine.

'Cheers!' I said, and for a moment I completely forgot about Charlie. I grinned at Becky. Becky grinned back at me. We were having an adventure. The sun was out, and for the first time in my life I realized that I actually liked my sister.

Then she said, 'I wonder how long we've got.'

'What do you mean?' I said.

She stared at the tarmac and muttered, 'They were nasty people, Jimbo. We don't even know if Charlie's still alive.'

'Shut up,' I replied quietly. 'Please just shut up.'

We finished our ice creams, put our helmets back on, revved the engine and made our way back to the queue for the bridge.

# 11

# the bad step

On Skye we stopped at a Co-op for bread, biscuits, lipstick, strawberry jam and Cheddar cheese. Becky took out her mobile and found that she had no reception. We were now officially off the map.

We headed into the hills. There was a village or two. There was a car or two. But mostly there were mountains, grass, lochs, cattle, sheep, rock and more mountains. It looked like the Land That Time Forgot. If you closed your ears to the roar of the Moto Guzzi, you could imagine a brontosaurus lumbering out of a valley between two cloudy peaks.

I thought about the men in the expensive light-grey suits. I thought about Mr Kidd and Mrs Pearce. And I simply couldn't connect any of them with this place. I began to wonder whether it was all a mistake, whether the map was just a map, a leftover from a holiday spent exploring Scottish castles. I began to wonder whether

Charlie really was in Portugal. Or whether something worse had happened.

The light began to fail. I was tired and I wanted to sleep. But I knew that I wouldn't be able to sleep. Not here. Not without seeing Charlie again.

Eventually the road curved off a hill and made its way into the little fishing village of Elgol. Seeing houses on either side of the road, I felt less nervy. A bedroom light here. A flower garden there. It seemed almost normal.

We turned a last corner and Becky brought the bike to a halt on a tiny stone jetty which cut into the water. An old man was standing on the jetty tidying lobster pots and coiling ropes. Beside him, his cocker spaniel was sitting quietly, panting and scratching its ear with a paw.

Becky lifted her helmet and leaned back to speak to me. 'That's the way,' she said, pointing her gloved hand along the coast. 'Now, let's go and find somewhere to camp.'

The sky was purple and orange in the sunset. The mountains were silhouettes, like jagged strips of torn black paper laid against the sky.

'I want to go now,' I said with determination.

'Jimbo, you're barking mad,' said Becky. 'It's eight miles. It's a rocky path. It's getting dark.'

'You saw them in the flat, Becky,' I said. 'They'll be following us. I know they will. We can't waste any time.

113

We've got to help Charlie. I'm going. With you or without you.'

'All right, all right,' she grumped, getting off the bike and helping me to transfer our stuff from the panniers to the holdall. 'I'll come. Not that I've got any choice. Mum would murder me if I went back and said I'd lost you.'

'You're a pal,' I said, shaking her hand.

'I'm a moron,' she replied.

We'd just locked the bike, picked up the bag and started out for the footpath when we were greeted by the old man who'd been tending the lobster pots.

'Evening,' he said in a broad Scots accent.

'Evening,' we replied suspiciously.

'Ah, city folk,' he said, looking at my trainers and Becky's black nail polish. 'You'll no be walking in that get-up, will you? With the night coming down.'

'No. We're going to see a film,' snapped Becky. She was always rather touchy about her 'get-up'.

'Yes. We're walking,' I explained politely. I wanted to get away. I didn't want to stand around chatting to strangers.

'To Camasunary? Or all the way to Coruisk?' he asked.

Then, very slowly, he lifted his pipe to his mouth, so that the sleeve of his oilskin fell away to show a band on his left wrist. I stepped backwards.

'To Coruisk,' said Becky curtly, 'so we haven't got any time to waste chatting.'

I expected the old man to come and grab me by the scruff of the neck. I expected to see his fingers light up. But neither of these things happened. He smiled. Then he chuckled.

'Well, you enjoy yourselves,' he said. 'It's going to be a nice pitch-black night for a walk along the cliff path.' And with that, he turned and walked back up the road, the cocker spaniel trotting at his heels.

'The wristband . . .' I said to Becky.

'I saw it,' she replied.

'They know we're here,' I whispered, looking around to see if there was anyone within earshot, crouching behind a lobster pot or an upturned boat.

'Maybe,' said Becky. 'Maybe it was just a brass wristband, Jimbo. Like people wear. Maybe we're getting paranoid.'

'Maybe,' I said. But I was right. I knew it. He was one of them. The way he showed us the wristband. The chuckle. On the other hand, if he was one of them, then we were on the right track. Coruisk was important.

So why didn't he stop us? Perhaps he knew we wouldn't make it along the path in the dark. Perhaps he knew we would find nothing when we got there. Perhaps he knew there were others waiting to greet us at the far end, flexing their neon-blue fingers in the windy dark.

'Well,' said Becky, 'what are we waiting for?'

I fell into step behind her.

We didn't need the torch. The lobster fisherman was wrong. The night was not pitch-black. Ten minutes after we set off, threads of grey cloud dissolved to reveal a perfect full moon suspended above the sea. It felt like walking through a scene from *Son of Dracula*. But at least we could see where to put our feet.

A good job too. The path was narrow and stony and cut into the steep, scrubby cliff rising high above the water. We had to duck under gnarled trunks, clamber over boulders and move fallen branches out of our way. The sea lay to our left like a great sheet of beaten silver.

To our right, rocks, trees and bushes climbed up into the night sky.

Out in the bay an island floated like a great barnacled whale. Beyond it, the ocean, blackness and stars. Everything looked mind-bogglingly big. I was lonely and frightened, even with Becky in front of me. If we tripped and fell, we'd helter-skelter down into the icy water and be swept away. No one would ever know.

To make matters worse, my city-folk trainers were not made for trekking and I was getting a large and painful blister on my right heel. I stuffed the shoe with tissues, gritted my teeth and marched manfully onwards.

After two hours we reached the bay of Camasunary. The path dropped down and the cliff flattened out into a gentle, sloping meadow of spiky grass. We crested a small ridge and the beach lay in front of us. We crossed a tiny stream and stepped into the field.

'Jeez!' I said.

'Now that does my head in,' echoed Becky.

The field was full of rabbits. A hundred. Two hundred. I'd never been frightened of rabbits before. But this lot gave me the creeps, sitting there with their powder-puff tails and their spoony ears like something from a horror film called *Rabbit*.

'Let's keep going,' I said.

We began the second, more difficult section of the path.

Except there wasn't much of a path any more. There were rocks, nettles, thorns, trees and mud, and my blister was getting worse.

After half an hour of slipping, tripping, grumbling and hobbling we came to an unexpected halt. In front of us lay a smooth, steep face of blank rock covered in patches of moss, like a giant granite nose. No mud, no branches, no clumps of grass. Nothing. Starting high above our heads, it swooped down to a ragged edge hanging over the surface of the black water. The map called it 'The Bad Step'. You could see what the map meant.

'You first,' I said. 'You're older.'

'Thanks, Jimbo,' Becky replied. 'You're a real gentleman.'

We couldn't go up and round. And we couldn't go down and under. The slope was just too steep. We had to go over.

Becky shimmied up. I shimmied up behind her. We lay face-down on the rock, spread-eagled like sunbathing lizards, and shuffled gingerly sideways.

We were doing all right. My trainers were rubbish for walking but the rubber soles stuck to the rock pretty well. Sadly, the moss didn't. I was halfway across when I put my foot on a clump of the stuff, and as I shifted my weight it tore away beneath me.

I shot downwards, braked only by my knees, my fingers and the end of my nose. My heart stopped and my feet slid over the bottom edge into space. I heard Becky scream and closed my eyes, waiting for the inevitable plunge through the air onto the pointy rocks half submerged in the freezing water below.

I came to a sudden halt, my legs dangling in the empty air. My fingers were jammed into a crack that ran across the surface of the stone. It was a narrow crack and my fingers were hurting and I wasn't going to be able to hang on for long. I tried to swing my legs up onto the rock, but I was too far over.

'Jimbo!' shouted Becky. 'Hang on!' I looked up. She was shifting herself slowly down the giant nose towards me with the holdall looped over her shoulder.

'There's a crack,' I said, and at that moment one of my hands slipped free and I screamed.

The toe of Becky's boot found the crack. She took the holdall off her shoulder and lowered it down to me. 'Grab this!' I grabbed it. 'Now pull.'

She pulled. I pulled. The handle stretched horribly. I

swung my right leg. Once. Twice. Three times. Finally, I got it over the lip of the rock. I heaved again and pulled. She heaved again and I got my other foot over the lip and lay flat against the slope, panting.

'Crikey, Jimbo,' she said. 'Don't do that to me again. Ever.'

We waited until we'd got our breath back, then started shuffling sideways, with our toes in the crack. We rounded the curve of the rock and were able to grab a gnarly root and swing ourselves onto the safety of the damp earth.

'Holy hotdogs, Batman,' said Becky. 'That was a close call.'

I put my hand to my face and realized that my nose was bleeding where I'd used it as a brake-pad.

'Well,' she said, 'you don't get this kind of excitement at school, do you?'

Coruisk caught us by surprise. The path led down to sea-level, where we found our way blocked by a little channel leading to the shore. We turned and followed the channel inland. We crossed over a rocky hump and the loch loomed into view, several billion gallons of cold dark water stretching away in front of us.

'Coruisk,' said Becky, standing on the rocky hump like someone who had just climbed Everest. 'We did it, kiddo.'

Around the loch on every side the Cuillin Hills rose into the night. The central strip of water shone blue in the moonlight, but the distant banks vanished in the soot-black shadows of the peaks. High above us plumes of mist were forming on the very tips of the mountains and trailing off into the star-filled sky.

The sea had seemed big, stretching out to the dark horizon. But the size of the silhouetted mountains made the loch seem even bigger. The silence was complete. There were waves on the sea. And the sound of water lapping against rock. The water here was as smooth and motionless as mercury. This was not a place where human beings were meant to be after dark.

'So,' said Becky, 'what do we do for our next trick?'

I thought about Charlie. 'I don't know.' I could feel tears pricking at the corners of my eyes. We'd spent two days getting to this place. We'd risked our lives at least twice. I didn't know what I was expecting to find when we got here. But I expected to find something at least. And this was the emptiest place I'd seen in my entire life.

'Chin up,' said Becky. 'Let's fix ourselves some dinner.'

# boom!

We trudged along the edge of the channel, crossed over using a series of stepping stones and looked for a good camping spot. En route we found the ruins of an old cottage that for a few seconds looked as if it might offer some kind of clue as to why Coruisk was so important. But it was just a ruin. Four crumbling walls, a doorway, two window holes, a mud floor. We climbed up to a flat area of grass, neatly protected from prying eyes and the growing wind by a large oval boulder.

Becky erected the tent behind the big stone. I got out some plasters and antiseptic wipes and Savlon and did first aid on my heel and my nose. Once we were snuggled into our sleeping bags we broke out the bread and cheese.

Well fed and footsore, we lay on our backs looking up at the stars through the open tent flap. Becky jammed her iPod earphones in and listened to some Evil Corpse. Or Gangrenous Limb. Or Dead Puppy. Or whatever else she'd downloaded recently.

I tried to remember the names of the constellations. The Bear. The Plough. Orion. Finally, I zipped up the tent, pulled the sleeping bag round my neck and closed my eyes.

'Uh-uh-uh-uh,' moaned Becky tunelessly. Then she stopped. She took one of the earpieces out of her ear, shook it, stuck it back in and tore it out again. I could hear a strange bubbling noise coming out of the tiny white speaker. 'It's broken,' she snapped. 'Again.'

'Your watch,' I gasped. 'Look at your watch.'

She looked at her watch. The face had lit up and the hand was spinning backwards.

'Ouch,' she yelped, ripping it off her wrist. 'It's hot.'

Somewhere inside the holdall, the torch was turning on and off.

Two seconds later the whole tent was bathed in a brilliant blue light.

# 12

# taking the tube

This was why the old man had chuckled. They were out there. He didn't have to get rid of us. His friends would do that. At Coruisk. Miles from anywhere. And there would be no one to save us.

I looked at Becky. She was white. And she was shaking. Or I was. It was hard to tell. It was the middle of the night. But under the canvas it looked like lunch time. In Greece. In summer.

'Becky,' I said, 'I'm going outside.' I had to see what was going on. I had to know who, or what, was out there and what it was planning to do to us. And if there was an opportunity to run, I wanted to run.

'Wait for me.' Becky reached into her pocket, pulled out a large penknife, opened the blade and crouched beside me, next to the zip.

I opened the tent. The unearthly blue light poured through the slit and we had to shield our eyes.

We stuck our heads out and looked up.

'Flipping heck!' muttered Becky.

There was a vast column of blue light, thick as a tube train, going straight upwards into the night sky. I wormed my way out of the tent and crouched in the shadow of the boulder. Becky crouched behind me. Together, we stood up slowly and peered over.

Even from thirty metres away we could feel the heat. The base of the column was rising out of the ruined cottage we'd passed earlier, making the crumbling stones shine so brightly they looked radioactive. Above the ruin, waves of brightness whisked upwards at high speed away from the ground. I took hold of Becky's arm for some small comfort.

Suddenly, there was an ear-splitting *boom!* like no *boom!* I'd ever heard. It made my head wobble. It made my stomach wobble. It made my toes wobble. The light went off. The *boom!* echoed back off the faraway mountains and slowly died away to silence. All we could hear was the blood thumping in our ears.

When my heart slowed down a bit I turned to Becky. 'Well, I guess this has to be the place.'

'Look,' whispered Becky, pinching my arm. 'Down there.'

I followed her eyes to the narrow channel connecting the loch to the sea. A silhouetted man was walking over the rocky ground towards the ruin. Behind him a little boat was moored in the channel, with a second silhouetted man on board.

The first man reached the ruin, turned, waved to the man in the boat and stepped inside. We heard the cough of an outboard motor being started up and the boat pulled away from the shore. There was a short fizzing noise and once again the column of brilliant blue light shot up out of the ruin into the sky.

'Oh my God!' said Becky.

The man had walked into the ruin. He had to be toast now. I was dreaming. I had to be dreaming.

The light shone. The waves of brightness whisked upwards. The *boom!* boomed. My toes wobbled. The light went off. The *boom!* echoed round the valley. And silence returned.

I gagged a bit. 'We just saw someone being killed, right?'

'Eeuw!' said Becky. 'That was not good.'

'We have to go down there,' I said.

'Why?' asked Becky.

'Because . . . because . . .' I said. 'Because that's the thing. That's the reason we're here. We can't sit here just looking at it.'

'No,' said Becky. 'I didn't bring you all this way so you could be cooked alive.'

'So what are we going to do?'

'We're going to sit here and look at it. See if it happens again.'

So we just sat there looking at it. For a long time. A very long time. And it didn't happen again. Becky wandered off to pee and came back again. I fell asleep and woke up when the pins and needles got really bad.

'OK,' said Becky. 'Let's go and take a look. This is driving me nuts.'

We did a commando shuffle through the dark. Down the slope from one shadow to the next. A tree. A rock. A bank of earth.

I thought about Dad, the model planes and the Aubergine Parmesan. I thought about Mum and her natty suits. I thought about my little room with the octopus poster and the cardboard skeleton. I thought about gravity and the Industrial Revolution. It all seemed a very long way away. Like something happening in a model village, tiny and silly and not quite real.

It wasn't fear. It was something way past that. It was

like walking away from a car accident. I felt shocked and spacey and full of adrenaline.

We reached the back wall of the ruin and crouched down. And that was the weird thing. The stones were cold.

There was no noise from inside, either. I looked at Becky. She looked back at me. The blade of her penknife flashed in the starlight.

She nodded and mouthed the word, 'Go.'

We stood up, tiptoed round to the front of the ruin and leaped through the hole that used to be the front door.

The place was completely empty. Moonlit walls. Dirty flagstones. Some weeds. Some little flowers. Nothing burned. No scorched earth. No crispy little person-remains. Nothing. It was just like it had been when we passed it earlier that night.

Dead or not, the man had vanished. I looked up. Had the blue beam vaporized him? What would happen to us if it came on again? Would we be vaporized too?

'Becky,' I said nervously, 'maybe we shouldn't hang around in here.'

She wasn't listening. 'There has to be a way out. A hidden door. A secret hatch.'

'Becky, please.' I tugged at her sleeve.

She scraped the floor with her boot. She ran her hand

over the stone walls. She ferreted among the scraggy plants growing in the corners.

'I'm leaving,' I said. 'I really don't like this place.'

'Give me the wristband.'

'I'm not sure that's a good idea.'

'Yeah?' said Becky. 'Well, you think of a better one. In the meantime, give me the wristband.'

I gave her the wristband.

It happened as soon as she peeled back the silver foil. The interior of the ruin was illuminated by fifty pinpricks of green light set into the stone walls. Beside the door a panel had appeared.

I snatched the wristband back and wrapped it up in its foil again.

'There's a button,' said Becky.

'Just don't press it.'

'Oh, right,' said Becky. 'So we're just going to stand here and look at it. That's not going to get us very far, is it?'

She pressed the button. The floor beneath my feet dropped away and I found myself being lowered into a round shaft.

'Help!'

'Jimbo!' yelled Becky. She threw herself onto the ground and grabbed my hand, but I was falling too quickly and our fingers were pulled apart.

# boom!

She stood up again and jabbed frantically at the button. It was too late. A thick plate was sliding over my head, cutting off the hole and shutting out the light. I banged on the walls and yelled.

Above me, I could hear Becky grunting as she struggled with the covering to absolutely no effect. A striplight came on over my head. I looked around. I was standing in a tall white ceramic tube. The walls were smooth as glass and on one side was a panel of buttons, dials, screens and gauges. Above me, the tube was sealed tightly by the steel plate.

'Jimbo . . . ! Jimbo . . . ! Jimbo . . . !' came the muffled sound of Becky's voice.

I gazed at the panel of buttons. Maybe one of them opened the door. But which one? And what were the others for? Press the wrong one and I might be microwaved, or crushed. The tube might fill with water. Or sulphuric acid. Or cockroaches.

I was finding it difficult to breathe. Was I running out of air, or just hyperventilating? I fumbled in the pocket of Craterface's jacket and took out his spanner. I bashed the wall as hard as I could. It clanged like a church bell and my fingers hurt. I hadn't made a scratch.

I put the spanner back, took out the wristband and unwrapped it. Instantly the panel came alive. Figures and symbols flashed up on a blue screen. Needles shook and quivered. Buttons glowed.

'Jimbo . . . ! Jimbo . . . !' Becky was still shouting faintly.

'I'm still here,' I shouted back. 'I'm trying to get out.'

I wrapped the wristband in its foil and put it back into my pocket. Then I picked up the orange notebook. I opened it at the page where Charlie had written down the code from Pearce's attic: *Trezzit/Pearce/4300785.*

The map reference was Coruisk. This was Coruisk. Perhaps the other numbers meant something too.

'Jimbo . . . !' shouted Becky, her voice dulled almost to silence by the ceiling of the tube.

I crossed my fingers and punched the numbers into the main keypad. 'Four . . . three . . . zero . . . zero . . . seven . . . eight . . . five . . .'

The word 'Pearce' flashed briefly on the screen, followed by a spurt of letters and symbols. I heard a low throb coming from machinery beneath my feet.

I pressed my back against the curved wall. I zipped up Craterface's jacket, braced my feet, took a deep breath and held on tight.

Nothing happened for several seconds. Then I heard the *boom!* Except it was much closer and much louder this time. I thought my ears were going to rupture. Every atom in my body was vibrating. I felt horribly seasick. My clothes were soaked in sweat. I covered my ears with my hands and fell to the floor and curled up into a ball.

The atoms in my body slowly stopped vibrating. My ears still hurt, but the nausea was fading. I got slowly to my feet. The word ZARVOIT flashed across the screen and there was a short *bing-bong* like a doorbell. I heard a little hiss and turned to see that one of the sides of the tube was sliding open.

The tube had gone downwards. I was in a cellar. Or a bunker. Except that there was light pouring through the gap, and it was white and it was bright and it was very much not underground. I gripped the spanner tightly.

It wasn't real. It couldn't be. I was looking out into a vast white hangar. I looked up. No Coruisk. No Becky. No ground. Just a smooth white ceiling twenty metres above my head.

Around the room were huge, high windows. Outside the windows was a black sky thick with stars. This wasn't a dungeon. This wasn't a cellar or a bunker. I must have travelled through some kind of tunnel. I was somewhere else on Skye. Or I was on the mainland. Or I was on that whale-shaped island sitting in the bay.

And that's when I saw them. Seated at a long table nearby. Mrs Pearce. Mr Kidd. The man from Captain Chicken. Inspector Hepplewhite. They were all wearing long violet robes.

This could not be happening. A few more minutes and the alarm would start beeping and I'd head into the kitchen and there would be a big cooked breakfast waiting for me. Sausages, toast, scrambled eggs.

Captain Chicken stood up and started walking towards me.

'Sausages, toast, scrambled eggs,' I said to myself. 'Sausages, toast, scrambled eggs.'

'Welcome, James,' he said, 'and well done. Well done indeed.'

The spanner fell out of my hand and clanged on the floor. There was no cooked breakfast. This was really happening.

'Fantabangle,' said Mr Kidd to Mrs Pearce.

'Mockety,' said Mrs Pearce to Mr Kidd. 'Parlant mockety.'

Captain Chicken grasped my hand and shook it. 'I think we're all agreed. You are precisely the kind of person we need.'

'A very enterprising young man,' said Inspector Hepplewhite.

'My name is Vantresillion, by the way,' said Captain Chicken. 'Bantid Vantresillion.'

I finally rediscovered my voice. 'Where am I?'

'The Sagittarius Dwarf Elliptical Galaxy.'

'What!?'

'It's about seventy thousand light years from the centre of your Milky Way Galaxy,' said Captain Chicken. 'In the direction of the Large Magellanic Cloud.'

'What!?' He was insane.

'It's often confused with the Sagittarius Dwarf Irregular Galaxy,' he said. 'By you, I mean. Not by us. The Sagittarius Dwarf Irregular Galaxy is, oh . . . much further away. Now . . .' He rubbed his hands together. 'You'll be in need of some sleep, unless I'm very much mistaken.'

He turned and waved his hand over some kind of red sausage sitting on the table. I heard a *pop!* from behind me and turned round.

And this was when I realized I might not be somewhere else on Skye, or on the mainland, or on the whale-shaped island. Because there was a spider walking towards me. A huge spider. About the size of a golden retriever. With the face of a squashed monkey.

I squealed and stepped backwards.

'Don't worry,' said Captain Chicken. 'It's completely harmless.'

The giant monkey-spider walked up to me and held out a hairy leg. 'Shake it, baby!'

I heard myself making a low, moaning noise.

'My name is Ktop-p-páãçôñïî,' said the spider. 'It will make a car crash in your mouth. But you can call me Britney.'

'Go with the spider,' said Vantresillion. 'It'll show you to your room.'

The spider pressed a hairy leg into the small of my back and pushed me gently towards the door. 'Ticket to ride!'

# 13

# short hairy tails

**W**e went out into the corridor, turned left and started walking. I tried very hard not to look at the spider. Everything was white and smooth and hi-tech. There were no lights. The ceiling just glowed a bit. There were no doors. The walls just opened up every so often so that people in purple robes could enter and exit.

'This way,' said Britney.

We turned a corner.

'You come from Earth,' said Britney, trotting beside me. 'I hear it is most delicious. Tell me about bagpipes. Tell me about Buckingham Palace and Elvis Presley. Tell me about cross-Channel ferries and ABBA, who are a Swedish pop band that shake my booty.'

'Where's Charlie?'

'Who is Charlie?' said Britney.

We walked in silence for a few more minutes.

'Does my English sparkle?' said Britney. 'Do we groove? Speak it to me from the hip. You are the horse's mouth. You eat the Yorkshire pudding.'

I was very tired. I needed sleep and I wasn't in the mood for an argument. 'Yes, you groove.'

'Disco inferno!' said the giant monkey-spider, waving two legs in the air.

We turned another corner and the white walls gave way to glass. We were walking across some kind of covered bridge between one building and the next. I stopped and looked out. And actually it was even scarier than seeing Britney for the first time. Because all around us, in every direction, stretched a barren, brown desert. No trees, no grass, no water. Just rocks and dust and craters. I turned to look out the other side of the bridge. And what I saw was much, much worse. There were two suns. And they were green. And they were revolving slowly around one another.

I staggered backwards and grabbed the handrail to stop myself falling over. 'So, this is . . .'

'Sagittarius Dwarf Elliptical Galaxy,' said Britney. 'Ten out of ten.'

'But . . . but . . . but . . . How did I get here?'

'No idea.' Britney held up two hairy legs. 'My brain is small.'

'So this place . . . this planet . . . it's . . .'

'Plonk.'

'Sorry?'

'Plonk.' Britney waved a leg over the barren landscape. 'It is the name.'

'Plonk!?' I said. 'That is the most stupid name for a planet I have ever heard.'

Britney looked decidedly huffy. 'It is a most serious and shiny name in our language.'

'Oh.'

'You have one called Moon,' said Britney. 'That is our word for passing wind out of the bottom. Now follow me.'

'So those people . . .' I said. 'Mrs Pearce and Vantrethingy . . .'

'Not human,' said Britney. 'Short hairy tails and no belly buttons.'

I thought of Mrs Pearce with a short hairy tail and it made me feel a bit ill. So I decided to stop asking questions.

'Whoa there!' said Britney.

We'd stopped by a section of wall with the words ARRIVALS UNIT on it. Britney said, 'Snekkit,' there was a *pop!* and a door appeared in the wall. 'Through here.'

We stepped into another corridor. The people here looked almost normal. None of them were wearing purple robes. Most were wearing jeans and T-shirts. There was a DOCTOR WHO T-shirt. There was a XENA WARRIOR PRINCESS T-shirt. One woman with large bosoms was wearing a T-shirt which said SET LASERS TO STUN.

'Your room,' said Britney. 'Snekkit!' The wall opened with a *pop!* 'Go in, human boy.' She was obviously still huffy about the Plonk thing.

I stepped inside. There was a white bed. There was a white chest of drawers. There was a white cubby hole containing a white toilet and a white sink.

Britney said, 'Snore now. Door locking.' There was another *pop!* and the door disappeared. 'Hey!' I banged on the hard white surface. I shouted, 'Snekkit!' thirty times at different volumes in different accents, but all to no avail.

I sat down on the bed, exhausted. On top of the chest of drawers was a kettle and a selection of tea bags and prepacked biscuits, just like in a bed and breakfast.

In the first drawer was a small library of boy books: SAS memoirs, football annuals, superhero comics . . .

In the third drawer there was nothing except some coloured balls the size of large marbles. I picked a few up. As I was doing this, I dropped one. A red one. Except it didn't drop. It just stuck in the air. I reached out and gingerly touched the ball. I could move it easily, but it wouldn't fall. It was like pushing a coin around a table, except in three dimensions. Wherever I shoved it, it simply hung there motionless.

The other balls were the same. I could arrange them in mid-air in any shape I chose. A line. A cube. A smiley face. I put five of them in my pocket. I couldn't wait to show them to Charlie.

Charlie. I'd forgotten about Charlie. I felt a stab of guilt. He was here somewhere. Probably. I hoped. And here I was mucking about with floaty balls and thinking how cool they were.

I had to find him. Except the door was locked and I was shattered. In the morning. Yes, I'd find him in the morning. But right now . . .

I laid my head down on the pillow. It was amazingly soft and comfortable. I was asleep in seconds.

# 14

# little blue suckers

I was sitting in the kitchen with Mum and Dad and Becky. Charlie was there too and we were eating lasagne and it was really, really good lasagne. Except someone was shaking my shoulder, so I rolled over and opened my eyes and screamed.

'Shift your potatoes,' said Britney.

I sat up and rubbed my eyes.

'How is the small one this morning?' asked Britney. 'Are your feelings good?'

'Of course my feelings aren't good. I'm on some stupid planet called Plonk in the . . . in the . . . in the Dancing Hamster Galaxy. And I'm talking to a monkey-faced spider called Britney.'

'Beastly child,' said Britney. 'Get walking. I will take you to breakfast. Put some food in your talk-hole.'

boom!

I made her wait outside while I went to the loo, then she led me through a maze of white corridors to a huge circular hall filled with people. The T-shirt people, not the purple robe people. There was a high domed roof and curving, star-filled windows, and everyone was milling and chatting and eating at long tables. It was like a massive school dining room, with space outside and giant monkey-spiders clearing away the dirty plates.

A middle-aged man with a flowery Hawaiian shirt and a ponytail wandered up to us. 'You must be a new guy.' He held out his hand. 'Bob Smith. Pleased to meet you.'

I didn't shake it.

'Take him,' said Britney. 'He hurts my head.' And with that she turned and scuttled away.

Bob Smith was still holding out his hand.

'Where's Charlie?' I said.

'Who's Charlie?'

'I want to see my friend. And there is no way I am going to shake the hand of some hairy-tailed, kidnapping alien with no belly button.'

Bob laughed. 'I'm human. Like you. Assuming you're human.'

'Oh. Sorry.' I shook his hand. 'Jimbo. My name's Jimbo.'

'You'll be hungry,' he said. 'Coming up the Weff-Beam really takes it out of a guy. Let's get you some tucker.'

I followed him to a round table at the edge of the room. Sitting on the table were a number of little blue suckers. He picked one up. 'Stick it onto your forehead.'

'What?'

'You think of a type of food and it . . . well, it appears. It's totally brilliant. Look.' He pressed a disc to his own forehead and grimaced like he was doing his thirteen times table. There was a *ping!* and a plate of scampi and a pint of lager appeared magically in the centre of the table. He picked them up.

'You have a go,' said Bob. 'You can get anything. Absolutely anything. You can get vomit if you want. Most people try it once. But it annoys everyone. You know, the smell.' He chuckled merrily. 'Oh, and trust me. There is nothing you can do to badger to make it taste good. Baking, boiling, stewing, puff pastry, batter . . . I've tried.'

I put the sucker to my head and tried very hard to clear my mind. If I wasn't careful I was going to get a serving of badger in vomit. 'Brie and marmalade sandwich,' I said to myself. 'White bread. No crusts. Brie and marmalade sandwich. White bread. No crusts. And some hot chocolate.'

There was another *ping!* and suddenly there it was. Brie and marmalade sandwich. White bread. No crusts. Mug of hot chocolate. Creepiest of all, the hot chocolate was in my battered Captain Scarlet mug. Or something that looked very like it.

'Come on,' said Bob. 'Let's find us a seat.'

We sat down and I took a bite of the sandwich. It tasted a bit like Brie and a bit like marmalade and a bit like petrol.

'Yeah,' said Bob. 'It's not perfect, but' – he looked around – 'is this whole place not totally the most incredible thing? I mean, we're on another planet, man.'

'No,' I said. 'Totally the most incredible thing would be finding my best friend and going home.'

'You're not into the whole sci-fi trip, then?'

'Look. No. Wait.' I was holding my head. This was all too much. Seventy thousand light years. The hairy tails.

The disco spiders. 'I mean . . . what the hell is going on?'

'It does kind of throw you a bit, doesn't it?' said Bob, chewing a mouthful of scampi. 'At first, I mean.'

'Yeah. It does. A bit.'

'They can't have children,' said Bob. 'Some kind of genetic malfunction.'

'I don't understand.'

'Fifty years and they'll all be dead.' Bob washed the scampi down with a swig of lager. 'So they decided to repopulate the planet.'

'By stealing people from Earth?'

'We're, like, the closest match. I mean, there's a lot of intelligent alien species out there. But some of them are seven hundred miles long, and some of them look like snot.'

I looked around the room. 'But everyone seems really happy about it. Don't they have, like, families and jobs and friends and stuff?'

'They're sci-fi fans,' said Bob. 'Clever, eh? You know, choosing the kind of people who'd really dig this place.'

'Hang on,' I said. 'They're going to populate a whole planet with sci-fi fans? Is that sensible?'

'I guess you must be an accident,' said Bob.

And that's when I saw him. Hunched over a table on the far side of the room. I'd have recognized him anywhere.

# boom!

I leaped to my feet, spilling hot chocolate and sending Brie and marmalade flying and shattering the Captain Scarlet mug on the floor.

'Easy, tiger!' said Bob.

'Charlie!' I shouted. 'Charlie!'

I ran across the room, tripping over the legs of a giant monkey-spider carrying a stack of crockery. 'Tighten your pants!' it shouted.

Charlie spun round in his seat. 'Jimbo!' He jumped off his bench and ran towards me and I don't think I've seen anything quite so wonderful in my entire life.

'Charlie!'

'Jimbo!'

We threw our arms round one another and jumped up and down and spun around whooping.

'Charlie!' I said. 'It is so good to see you!'

He grinned. 'I knew you'd make it, Jimbo. I just knew it.'

'You're here!' I said. 'I didn't even know whether you were alive.'

'So,' said Charlie, sitting down again, 'did they capture you or what?'

'No, no, nothing like that. We knew they'd got you. And they tried to get me too. The guy with the suit. And these other men.'

'Uh-huh,' said Charlie.

'But Becky and Craterface, they turned up at the flat and Craterface fought them off and Becky and I borrowed Craterface's motorbike.'

'Uh-huh,' said Charlie.

Something was wrong. He wasn't excited enough. He wasn't interested enough. Maybe it was shock. Maybe it was the petrol-flavoured food. I carried on. 'But the important thing is, we've got to find a way out of here.'

'Actually,' said Charlie, 'I think I'm going to stay.'

'What!?'

'Look at this place. It's brilliant.'

'What!?'

'They've got hover-scooters. I bet you haven't seen the hover-scooters yet.'

'No, listen,' I said. 'Shut up about the stupid hover-scooters. I came all this way to help you escape, so—'

'That's really good of you,' said Charlie. 'But I like it here. I really do.' His voice was calm and he was smiling like he'd become a member of a weird religious cult.

I stood up and leaned across the table. 'Shut up, you idiot. I nearly died looking for you. Your mum and dad are going out of their minds. And now my mum and dad will be going out of their minds.'

# boom!

'Give it a few days,' said Charlie in the same creepy, chilled-out way. 'It really grows on you.'

I slumped back down onto my seat. 'They've brain-washed you, haven't they? They've given you drugs. Or put electrodes into your brain. They've turned you into a zombie.'

Charlie laughed. 'Of course they haven't. You're just suffering from jet-lag. Trust me.'

I was too angry to speak. I grabbed him by the collar and shook him hard. 'You're meant to be my friend! You're meant to be my friend!'

'Hey, hey, hey,' said Charlie. It was the same grown-up voice Mum and Dad used when I was getting upset. 'It's going to work out fine.'

'Fine!?' I swung my fist and hit him as hard as I could.

'Ouch!' He put his hand to his face and took it away again. There was actual blood.

I pushed him backwards so that he fell to the ground. Then I turned and ran.

# 15

# orange toilet plungers

reached the edge of the room. I was about to shout 'Snekkit!' and leap through the door when the lights went out and the entire dining hall went dark. I skidded to a halt. I could see absolutely nothing.

I expected people to start screaming, but all I could hear were excited *Ooohs* and *Aaahs* that died away to a hushed silence. There was a distant whirring noise and a line of soft white light fell across the middle of the room.

I looked up and saw the roof opening like a huge eye to reveal an enormous glass dome. Beyond the dome lay a trillion miles of darkness filled with twinkling stars.

Bob appeared beside me. 'I saw that thing back there. The bust-up with your friend. That was a seriously bad trip, man.'

'What's happening?' I said. 'I mean, the roof and everything.'

'Wait and see,' said Bob. 'It's kinda mind-boggling.'

# boom!

The whirring stopped. The roof was now fully open. Way over to my right the two green suns were revolving slowly around one another. Over to my left . . .

'Here comes the ferry,' said Bob.

'The what?'

'The intergalactic ferry,' said Bob. 'Goes round all the neighbouring star systems. Picks up passengers and cargo and stuff.'

A vast object began to slide into view. A spaceship. A real live spaceship. Antennae and gantries and rockets and pods and fins and tubes. Moving as slowly as an oil tanker but a hundred times the size.

'The scorch marks are from jumping in and out of hyperspace,' said Bob. 'It gets pretty hot. And look at the front. You can see the asteroid bumper. That huge panel with all the dents in.'

There was a deep and distant rumble. You could feel the floor vibrating gently.

'Cool or what?' said Bob.

'Cool,' I said. 'Definitely cool.'

'It's not home,' said Bob. 'There's no football on the telly and the scampi's a bit rubbish. But if you're going to spend the rest of your life on another planet, then this one's not a bad choice.'

He was right. Of course he was right. I was lucky. I was alive. I should be grateful.

There was a faint shooshing noise and little tongues of orange flame flickered from twenty rockets down the side of the intergalactic ferry.

'Final adjustments,' said Bob. 'You know, before coming into dock.'

'Wow.'

We stood in silence, watching the ferry fly slowly over the dome until the last tail-fin disappeared and we were left staring up into the night sky.

The lights clicked back on and everyone covered their eyes while they got used to the brightness. The roof began whirring shut and the chatter started up again. Then I heard someone whispering, 'Smelly fart,' in my ear, which was quite odd.

I turned and found myself looking at Charlie. 'Smelly fart,' he said again. 'Gordon Reginald Harvey Simpson Bennett Junior and walkie-talkies and raspberry pavlova. I'm still Charlie. Just . . . come and sit down and talk to me, OK?'

'Shut up.'

'Jimbo, please. Just . . .'

He was still Charlie. Whatever they'd done to him. I couldn't carry on being angry for ever. 'I'll come,' I said. 'But don't give me any more twaddle about how you're staying here, or I swear I'll brain you.'

'Promise,' said Charlie.

boom!

We walked back across the room and he sat me down while he went to get some more food.

Two women at the next table were arguing about whether Daleks were scarier than Cybermen. It puzzled me. The inhabitants of Plonk were meant to be super-intelligent. They had hover-scooters. They had a ferry that went through hyperspace. Why didn't they repopulate their planet with engineers? Or fighter pilots? Or accountants?

Charlie came back carrying a huge bowl containing an industrial volume of tinned spaghetti in tomato sauce. The smell was not good.

He stuck his spoon into the bowl and started fiddling and stirring. Like those kids at school who don't really enjoy eating, but love building snowmen out of mashed potatoes and smiley faces out of peas. I wanted to tell him to grow up and actually talk to me. But it was good sitting here with him, and if he didn't say anything I could just about pretend they hadn't done anything to his brain.

At last he stopped playing with his spaghetti. 'Try some,' he said, pushing the bowl towards me.

'No way,' I said. 'I hate spaghetti.'

'Yes,' said Charlie. 'But this spaghetti is *special* spaghetti.' He had the weird, religious-cult-member face on again.

'Charlie,' I said, trying to control my rising frustration, 'I don't like spaghetti. And you know I don't like spaghetti because the last time I ate a tin of spaghetti I barfed the whole thing up. And you know I barfed the whole thing up because I barfed it up all over you.'

Charlie rubbed his forehead and took a deep breath and looked at me and squeezed his face up like he was having serious trouble on the toilet. 'Jimbo, this is *alphabetti* spaghetti.'

'You're eating alphabetti spaghetti?' I said. 'Well, that's really reassuring. Are you seven years old?'

'Just look at the bowl!' said Charlie.

'No,' I said, folding my arms.

Charlie stood and leaned across the table and shouted, 'How thick are you!? Of course I hate this place. Of course I want to escape. And I had a brilliant plan. But you have totally screwed it up by being a total, total moron. Look at the bloody bowl!'

I looked at the bowl. The letters of the spaghetti were arranged to read:

# shut up
# theyre
# listening
# to us

'Oh,' I said. 'That's why you were acting weird.'

'Yes,' said Charlie sarcastically. 'That's why I was acting weird.'

'Because you wanted them to think you really liked it here.'

'Yes,' said Charlie sarcastically. 'Because I wanted them to think I really liked it here.'

'So,' I said, 'what happens to you if you don't like it here?'

'They fire you into space?' said Charlie. 'Or feed you into some kind of grinding machine? I have no idea. But it basically starts with a couple of armed spiders dragging you off screaming. Like this.'

He pointed over my shoulder. I turned round. Captain Chicken, aka Bantid Vantresillion, was standing

154

at the edge of the room in his violet robe, with two giant monkey-spiders at his side. The spiders were wearing crash helmets and carrying orange toilet plungers.

'Seize them!'

The giant monkey-spiders sprinted towards us.

'Run!' said Charlie.

We dodged and dived. We slid along benches and jumped over tables. I covered a woman in mushroom soup. Charlie sat in a bowl of treacle pudding. A spider raised a toilet plunger and a fizzing line of laser-light zapped past my leg, singeing my jeans. Charlie dodged a second one and it set fire to the hair of a sci-fi fan who was eating a knickerbocker glory.

'I love the nightlife!' shouted one of the spiders.

'Bumper cars!' shouted the second.

Somehow we made it to the main entrance. I shouted, 'Snekkit!' The wall opened up and we raced into the corridor.

I have to say we did pretty well. I don't think either of us had run that fast in our entire lives. At one point I shoved a fat guy off a hover-scooter and we both leaped on, but the joystick looked like a tomato and I had no idea how to use it so the scooter just sank to the floor with a squirty hiss. We leaped off and kept on running.

They caught us, of course. They had more legs and the deadly toilet plungers. So I guess we were pretty lucky they didn't fill us full of smoking holes. We ground to a halt and stood with our hands on our knees, puffing and wheezing. A couple of seconds later our arms and legs were wrapped in hairy brown tentacles. The spiders were surprisingly strong. And their breath was appalling.

'Snack them down!' said one of them. 'Alive! For freshness!'

'Foot on the brake!' said the other. 'We do not want the electric prod.'

'No,' said the first. 'We do not want the electric prod.'

Vantresillion appeared behind the spiders. 'Take them to the holding cell.'

'What are you going to do to us?' asked Charlie.

Vantresillion laughed, then turned and walked away.

'Come with us, little bald monkeys,' said the first spider.

We were lifted into the air and they scuttled off at high speed in the opposite direction, jiggling us up and down and not bothering at all about banging our heads on the walls when they went round corners.

Three minutes later they snekkited a door open and threw us into a small room and snekkited the door shut behind us.

This room was different. This room was not white. This room was grey and black and brown. The walls were made of something like concrete and they hadn't been cleaned for a couple of hundred years. There was brown goo running down them and a mess in the corner like something had died there quite recently.

'Lovely,' said Charlie.

We didn't say anything for a while.

I took a deep breath. 'Sorry, this was my fault.'

'It's OK,' said Charlie. 'I forgive you. Sort of.'

Once more we didn't say anything for a while.

'What was the plan?'

'The plan?' asked Charlie.

'Yeah,' I said. 'The brilliant plan. The one I screwed up by being a total, total moron.'

'Oh, that one,' said Charlie. 'Well, if you put those suckers on your forehead and think hard enough, you can make Brussels sprouts that go off like grenades when you throw them.'

'And . . . ?'

'I was collecting them,' said Charlie. 'You know, building up an arsenal, so I could fight my way out.'

'To where?' I said. 'We're seventy thousand light years from planet Earth. Unless you've got some Black Forest gateau that turns into a spaceship.'

'OK,' said Charlie. 'No need to be sarcastic. At least I was trying.'

There was a sinister grating noise from the other side of the wall.

'That's probably the grinding machine,' said Charlie. 'Thanks for coming to get me, by the way.'

I nodded. 'No problem. I mean, obviously I didn't have a choice. You being my friend and everything. Plus I missed you.'

'Yeah, me too. I think I'd have gone mad if you hadn't turned up. Everyone talking about *Blade Runner* and speaking Vogon.'

I don't know how long we were in the holding cell. The lights were on all the time and our watches hadn't worked since we arrived on Plonk. We talked about Megan Shotts and the locusts. We talked about Mr Kosinsky's snowman socks. We talked about salmon mousse, and strawberry jam and Cheddar cheese sandwiches.

But thinking about home made us sad. So we played noughts and crosses on the floor by scraping the dirt with the toes of our shoes. Then we tried to name all the countries in the world. Except we kept remembering that we were going to be killed, which was a bit distracting.

Ten hours passed. Or maybe twenty. Or thirty. We got really tired. We tried to lie down and sleep but it was hard to relax lying in brown goo. So we stood up again. And then we got so tired we didn't care about the brown goo any longer so we lay down and slept.

We hadn't been asleep for long when we were woken by two more giant monkey-spiders. Or maybe it was the same ones. It was hard to tell.

'Do the locomotion,' said one.

'Walkies!' said the other.

'Are you going to execute us now?' asked Charlie.

'Hurrah,' said one. 'You are a clever boy.'

'We are the champions!' sang the other. 'But you're not.' Then it snickered gleefully.

We fought for a bit, but it was no use. They grabbed us by the arms and legs and hoisted us over their heads and hauled us off down the corridor.

Five minutes later we were taken into a hi-tech white office with blue rubber plants and Bantid Vantresillion sitting behind a desk. The giant monkey-spiders dropped us onto the floor.

'You may go now,' said Vantresillion and the spiders scuttled out.

# boom!

'Charles . . .' said Vantresillion. 'James . . .'

'Are you going to kill us?' asked Charlie again, getting to his feet.

'No,' said Vantresillion.

'But the spiders,' I replied, 'they told us . . .'

'They have a strange sense of humour,' said Vantresillion.

'Oh.'

'Normally we'd kill you,' said Vantresillion. 'But I think you may be able to help us.'

I felt a huge wave of relief and everything went a bit wobbly for a few seconds. But Charlie still had his head screwed on properly. 'Great,' he said. 'Just fire away and we'll see what we can do. We like being helpful, don't we, Jimbo?'

'Er, what?' I said. 'Yes, that's right. We like being helpful.'

'Hmmm,' said Vantresillion. 'I have a problem. Every time one of the Watchers travels to Skye to come back to Plonk we lose contact with them.'

'Plonk,' said Charlie, chuckling. 'That makes me laugh every time.'

'Charlie . . . ?' I said.

'What?'

'Don't be rude about their planet, all right?'

'Good idea,' said Charlie. So I reckon he was feeling a bit wobbly as well.

'And every time we beam someone down to find them, we lose contact with them too.'

'That'll be the army,' said Charlie. 'Or the police. Both, probably.'

'But no one knows about the Weff-Beam,' said Vantresillion through gritted teeth.

'Yeah, they do,' said Charlie. 'Jimbo told them, didn't you, Jimbo?'

'Did I?'

'It's OK,' said Charlie. 'You don't have to keep it secret any longer.'

'Right,' I said. I had no idea what Charlie was doing, but I had no other ideas so I decided to go along with it. 'Yeah. We had a notebook. And a map and stuff. From Mrs Pearce's attic. And I gave it to Mum and Dad. So they know all about the Weff-Beam thingy.'

'You're lying,' said Vantresillion.

'Scout's honour,' said Charlie, holding up three fingers. 'Cross my heart and hope to die.'

Come to think of it, he was probably right. Becky had seen the Weff-Beam. She'd go to the police. They'd have the place surrounded by now. Tanks, barbed wire, marksmen.

'I guess they're shooting them as they come up out of the ground,' said Charlie. 'Because they're aliens with tails.'

# boom!

'I have lost five Watchers,' said Vantresillion darkly. 'Any more and I swear I will kill everyone on your benighted little planet.'

'You're just kidding, aren't you?' said Charlie, smiling.

Vantresillion leaned over and pulled a black box into the centre of the desk. There were a series of buttons on the box. He placed his finger on the red one. 'I press this,' he said, 'and your planet blows up. No Eiffel Tower. No Great Wall of China. Just a load of smoking rocks in space.'

'What do the other ones do?' asked Charlie. 'Do they make cappuccino?'

I turned to him and scowled. 'Just try and be a bit nicer, OK? He might actually be telling the truth.'

'Look,' said Vantresillion. He spun round and a screen appeared on the wall. In the centre of the screen was a planet. Sort of like Saturn, with rings around it and three moons. 'Zip Seven,' said Vantresillion. 'We've got a Weff-Beam there too.' He pressed the yellow button. There was a loud bang and the planet erupted in a vast ball of fire.

'Holy cow!' said Charlie.

The planet was gone. Just a load of smoking rocks and three little moons drifting sadly off into space.

'My God,' I said. 'Were there, like, people on that planet?'

'Yes,' said Vantresillion. 'But they looked like squirrels and they were stupid and I didn't like them very much.' He took two brass wristbands from his desk and threw them to us. 'Put these on.'

We put them on. He pressed a third button and they snapped tight.

'Ouch!' said Charlie.

I tried to get mine off but it had shrunk and there was no way I could slip it over my hand.

'You go down on the Weff-Beam,' said Vantresillion. 'You talk to whichever moron is in charge down there and you tell them we want the Watchers back.'

'But . . .' said Charlie. I could hear the wheels spinning in his brain. 'They're not going to believe us. "The Earth is going to be blown up." It doesn't sound very convincing, does it?'

'Then you must be persuasive,' said Vantresillion. 'Snogroid!'

A door opened and a spider scuttled in. Vantresillion chucked the spider another wristband. 'Put this on.'

The spider put it on and we heard it snap tight. 'Delightful bangle,' it said. 'And most snug.'

Vantresillion turned back to us. 'You will have five minutes. Then you call me using the wristbands. If you have not solved the problem, then this happens to Charles.' He pressed the green button. There was

163

another bang and a hideous scream. The spider erupted in flames and the room was filled with brown smoke and the smell of burning hair. When the smoke cleared there was a ring of black ash on the floor and a buckled wristband, still glowing slightly from the heat.

'That should help change their minds,' said Vantresillion. 'Five more minutes and I will do the same to James. After that I will just lose patience and press the red button. Then I will press the last button and get a nice cappuccino.' He thought this was very funny and laughed for a long time. 'Now. Follow me.'

# 16

# the big knobbly stick

**V**antresillion strode down the corridor with us jogging behind him. He was carrying the button box and we were wearing the wristbands so there was no point in running away.

'Hey,' said Charlie. 'Look on the bright side. We're going home.'

'Except we'll only be there for five minutes, then we'll be dead.'

'No,' said Charlie. 'Then *I'll* be dead. You get another five minutes.'

'Brilliant. That makes me feel a lot better.'

'You never know,' said Charlie. 'Brigadier-General Doo-Dah might actually believe us.'

'No one ever believes us,' I said. 'About anything.'

'In here,' said Vantresillion. 'Snekkit.'

A door opened in the wall and we found ourselves in the large white hangar where I'd first arrived. The white ceiling twenty metres over our heads. The high windows with the starscape outside. Just as before, Pearce, Kidd and Hepplewhite were sitting at the long table in their violet robes.

'Tidnol,' said Vantresillion. 'Basky dark.'

'Crispen hooter mont,' said Mrs Pearce, standing up. She walked over to us. 'Well, well, well. You turn out to be useful after all. Now that is a surprise.'

'Always willing to help,' said Charlie.

'Get into the Weff-Beam unit,' said Vantresillion. 'And remember. Five minutes. Charles is dead. Ten minutes. James is dead. Then I get bored very, very quickly.'

He shoved us towards the tubular cubby hole. 'Inside. Both of you.'

'It's going to be a bit of a squash,' said Charlie.

'Getting squashed is the least of your problems,' said Vantresillion.

I stepped inside. Charlie stepped in beside me. Vantresillion pushed. Then he pushed a bit harder. Then he said, 'Snekkit,' and the curved door slid shut behind us.

'Fasten seatbelts,' said Charlie, his face pressed against my ear. 'Cabin doors to automatic.'

'So what's the plan?' I asked.

'Absolutely no idea,' said Charlie. 'If we're really lucky,

a paratrooper might kill us with a bazooka as soon as we come out of the ground.'

Then we heard the *boom!* and it was like being hit in the head with a cricket bat. I covered my ears with my hands and every atom in my body started vibrating. My clothes were soaked in sweat and I felt horribly seasick. Charlie must have felt seasick too, because he was actually sick down my back and it smelled really bad.

The atoms in my body stopped vibrating and the nausea started to fade. Charlie said, 'Sorry about that,' and the word ZARVOIT flashed across the little screen beside my head. There was a short *bing-bong* like a doorbell, the roof of the tube slid back and we began to rise upwards.

Sunlight. I could see actual sunlight. We rose a little further and I could see the tops of the mountains. And grass. Real grass.

And then I saw a crazed figure standing above us, with matted hair and mad, staring eyes and a huge knobbly stick in its hands. It yelled like Tarzan of the Apes and

# boom!

swung the stick and whacked Charlie. He screamed and rolled sideways into the grass, holding his shoulder.

Then the crazed figure with the matted hair and the mad, staring eyes and the huge knobbly stick said, 'Jimbo!' and I realized that it was Becky.

'Don't hit me!' I shouted.

'You're back!' shouted Becky. She grabbed me and hugged me, just like I'd done when I found Charlie in the dining hall. And I grabbed her and hugged her back. I don't think I'd ever been more pleased to see her.

'Baby brother!' she said.

'You waited for us,' I said.

'Of course I waited,' said Becky. 'What was I going to do? Go home and get killed by Mum and Dad for losing you? But where in God's name have you been? And why is your back covered in sick?'

Then I remembered. 'I'll explain everything later. We've got to stop the planet being blown up.'

'What!?' said Becky.

I looked around. 'Why aren't the army or the police here?'

'What the hell are you talking about?' said Becky. 'Now just calm down and tell me what happened to you.'

Vantresillion's voice appeared in my head. 'How are we doing, James? Three minutes to go. I'm tapping my fingers. Are you speaking with the person in charge?'

I touched my wristband. 'Er. Yeah. I'm speaking with the person in charge right now. We're going to sort something out. Very soon.' I took my fingers off the wristband.

'Who are you talking to?' asked Becky.

Charlie got to his feet. 'That really hurt.'

'Sorry,' said Becky. 'I thought you were one of them.'

'Becky. Wow. It's you,' said Charlie. 'I didn't recognize you with the cave-woman disguise.'

I turned to Becky. 'What do you mean, *one of them*?'

'That big blue light goes on,' said Becky. 'There's a *boom!* I wander over and whack them over the head. Then I tie them up behind that big rock over there. Where are they all coming from?'

'Ah,' said Charlie. 'You're the reason they've lost contact. Brilliant. Super-intelligent alien civilization foiled by a girl with a stick.'

'Charlie,' I said. 'Shut up. We haven't got much time.'

'Oh yeah,' said Charlie. 'I forgot. I'm still feeling a bit shaken. You know, on account of being assaulted.'

'There's no police,' I said. 'There's no army. What the hell are we going to do?'

Vantresillion's voice was in my head again. 'Two minutes to go. I'm getting twitchy here.'

Charlie was walking round in little circles, squeezing his head. 'OK. Think . . . Think . . . Think . . .'

'You haven't answered my question,' said Becky.

'Which question?' I said.

'Where in God's name have you been? I've been stuck here for six days living off loch water and Quality Street.'

'Six days?' I said.

'Yes,' said Becky. 'Six days.'

'That's funny,' I said. 'I thought we were only gone for a day. Something must have gone a bit strange with space-time.'

Becky grabbed me by the shoulders and shouted, 'Where in God's name have you been?'

I took a deep breath. 'Plonk. It's in the Sagittarius Dwarf Elliptical Galaxy. It's seventy thousand light years from the centre of the Milky Way. In the direction of the Large Magellanic Cloud.'

Becky shook her head. 'We have to get you to a doctor.'

'One minute to go,' said Vantresillion.

'Becky,' I said. 'Listen. This is important. It is very possible that, in about fifty seconds, Charlie is going to, like, explode.'

Becky stared at me with her mouth hanging open.

'Five minutes after that I'm going to explode too. So I just wanted to say that I love you. And don't stand too close to me. And a few minutes later . . . well, it's probably best not to think about that bit.'

'Thirty seconds . . .' said Vantresillion.

I walked over to Charlie and said, 'You're the best friend ever. You know that, don't you? And I sort of love you too. But not in a girly way.'

'Shut up!' said Charlie.

'Oh, OK, then,' I said huffily.

Charlie touched his wristband. 'Mr Vantresillion . . . ?'

I pressed my own wristband to listen in.

'Yes?' snapped Vantresillion.

There was a pause. 'We have a problem.'

'What?'

'The Watchers are all here,' said Charlie.

'Good,' said Vantresilllion.

'But they're tied up.'

'Well, untie them, you brainless idiot,' said Vantresil-lion.

'I'm standing next to a very large policeman,' said Charlie. 'And he's not keen on me doing that.'

'What the hell is going on?' asked Becky.

I clapped a hand over her mouth.

'Fenting Nard!' said Vantresillion. 'Get your friend to stand next to him so I can blow them up together.'

'You can't be serious,' said Charlie.

"Nnnnnnggg,' said Becky, trying to tear my hand away.

'Fenting, fenting, fenting nard!' said Vantresillion. 'Don't move. I'm sending someone down. And when they've

171

dealt with the very large policeman you are going to be *toast*! Do you understand?'

'Absolutely,' said Charlie and took his fingers off the wristband. He turned to Becky. 'Time for you to get your big stick.'

I took my hand off Becky's mouth and she said, 'Would you kindly tell me what is going on? And why is there an imaginary policeman? And who the hell are you talking to?'

But Charlie didn't get a chance to explain because the blinding blue light was pouring out of the sky. Then there was an ear-splitting *boom!* and the light went off and Becky picked up her big knobbly stick and ran over to the ruined cottage and lifted the stick over her head. The cover slid sideways and Mrs Pearce's head emerged from the hole and Becky hit it really hard with the stick and Mrs Pearce squealed and rolled sideways and lay face-down on the earth, completely unconscious.

'Oh my God,' said Becky. 'I've just hit a really old lady over the head.'

'Actually,' said Charlie, 'that's Mrs Pearce.'

'My God,' said Becky. 'I've just hit your history teacher over the head.'

I bent down and started lifting Mrs Pearce's skirt. 'This will make you feel better.'

'What the hell are you doing, Jimbo?' said Becky.

'I need to show you something.'

'You sick and twisted little boy,' said Becky. 'No way am I looking at a teacher's bottom.'

And there it was. Coming out of a neat little hole in the back of Mrs Pearce's knickers. A bit like a long hairy parsnip. The tail.

'Jeez,' said Charlie. 'That is going to be burned into my memory, like, for ever.'

'Becky,' I said. 'Open your eyes.'

'No.'

'Open your eyes.'

'No.'

'Open your eyes.'

Becky opened her eyes and looked down and screamed. Then everything was lit up by a bright blue light and the mountains rang with the deafening *boom!* – except we didn't take much notice because we were all so freaked out by Mrs Pearce's tail. And then we heard someone say, 'Little human scum!' and we spun round to see Vantresillion rising out of the Weff-Beam tube.

Becky ran towards him and lifted the big knobbly stick and swung it, but he was too quick. He grabbed the end and yanked it out of Becky's hands.

'Narking frotter!' he yelled, his eyes sparking with blue light. 'I am toasting you now.' He reached for his wristband.

# boom!

'Stop him!' shouted Charlie.

But Becky had already whipped a can of L'Oréal extra-strength hairspray from her back pocket and squirted him in the eyes. He screamed and raised his hands to his face and fell to the ground.

'The wristband,' I said and stamped on Vantresillion's arm while Charlie yanked it off and flung it as hard as he could. We stood and watched it sail through the air until it plopped into the water next to the little boat moored to the rocks.

Vantresillion said, 'Aaeeaaeeaaeeaargh!'

And Charlie said, 'Jimbo, your sister is one feisty chick.'

'I'm assuming that's a compliment,' said Becky.

'Yeah,' said Charlie. 'But when Vantresillion doesn't check in, someone is going to press that button and we're going to explode, so we have to do something spectacular in the next minute.'

Vantresillion got to his feet and staggered around blindly, trying to find us and strangle us.

'Petrol,' I shouted. 'There's petrol in the boat. We set light to the Weff-Beam thing. We blow it up.'

We ran down to the water's edge and tried to lift the outboard motor off the stern but it was too heavy.

'Forget that,' said Becky, holding a red plastic fuel can. 'This is what we need.'

We ran back up the grassy slope to the ruined cottage.

'It's closing!' shouted Charlie. 'Quick!'

I grabbed the broken knobbly stick and shoved it into the hole. It splintered and cracked. Charlie and Becky staggered over with a rock and jammed it into the gap. The mechanism squeezed and juddered and gave off a lot of evil brown smoke.

Becky screwed the black top off the red plastic can and poured the contents into the Weff-Beam unit. 'Now,' she said. 'Let's set light to it.'

'How?'

Becky paused for a moment. Then she said a really, really rude word. 'We haven't got a lighter!'

The mechanism juddered and smoked and the rock cracked into two pieces.

'Craterface's lighter!' I searched madly through the pockets. The cigarettes, the wallet, the oily fluff . . . and the lighter.

I threw myself to the ground and shoved my arm down past the lid.

'Stop, you moron!' shouted Charlie. 'You'll blow yourself to pieces!'

He ripped off his shirt and shoved the sleeve into the mouth of the petrol can, then pulled it out and set light to it. The rock finally shattered, Charlie shoved the flaming shirt through the last inch of shrinking gap and shouted, 'Run!'

We ran and hurled ourselves to the ground and waited. And waited. And absolutely nothing happened. Except for Vantresillion wandering into the ruined cottage, moaning, with his arms stretched out in front of him, clawing the air like a lost zombie.

He was standing in the very centre of the cottage when the blue light flashed on. He screamed again, but much, much louder this time. Then he vanished inside the column of light and we couldn't hear him screaming any more. Then the light went off and the *boom!* shook the mountains and we saw that Vantresillion had been turned into a smoking black statue of himself. One arm fell off and smashed on the ground. Then the head did the same thing.

'It didn't work!' said Charlie. 'It didn't—'

And then, suddenly, it *did* work. There was a shuddering *whump!* and the Weff-Beam unit and the cottage and the black statue of Vantresillion erupted in a massive cauliflower of orange flame. We closed our eyes and covered our heads. The heat wave hit us and it was like being run over by a really hot lorry.

We opened our eyes. There was an ominous silence for about two seconds, then a horrible clatter as broken pieces of highly advanced technology rained down around us. I looked up and rolled out of the way just in time to prevent myself being kebabbed by a long spear of ceramic tube-wall.

We got up and picked bits of ash and shrapnel off our clothing and walked back towards the ruin. Except it wasn't there any more. There was a black crater. There was a ring of charred stones. There were some wires. There was a triangle of cracked blue glass.

I heard a little click and felt my wristband loosen and fall to the ground. I heard another little click and saw Charlie's wristband do the same.

He bent down and picked them up. 'You know,' he said. 'Just to be on the safe side.' He drew back his arm and hurled them into the water.

And this was when we saw Mrs Pearce. She'd finally come round and got to her feet. She had her fingers pressed to her own wristband. 'Gretnoid,' she said. 'Nutwall venka berdang.' She pressed it again. 'Gretnoid. Nutwall venka berdang.' Her voice was getting more and more panicky. 'Gretnoid . . . ? Gretnoid . . . ?'

Charlie walked up to her. 'You've lost all contact with Plonk, haven't you?'

She growled at him.

'Brilliant,' said Charlie. 'I'm kind of assuming they can't blow us up now. Or the planet. Is that right?'

'You're going to suffer for this. I am going to make you

all suffer so very, very much.'

'How?' said Charlie.

She paused for a few moments, then she slumped to the ground and started to cry. 'Oh God,' she wailed. 'I'm going to be stuck on your stupid, primitive, godforsaken planet for ever.'

'Anyway,' said Becky, 'we're off now. There are five of your friends tied up over there. Behind the big boulder. They're going to need a bit of help.'

We walked back to the tent. The five Watchers were tied up nearby. I recognized two of them from the red Volvo. They were all a bit snarly at first. Then Charlie explained that the Weff-Beam had been destroyed and that they wouldn't be going home. After this they went a bit quiet. A couple of them cried, just like Mrs Pearce.

Becky dug around in the holdall and found a spare shirt for Charlie. We packed up and headed back down to the water. Mrs Pearce was still on her hands and knees, crying, when we walked past her.

'Cheerio!' said Charlie.

She looked up at him and whimpered like a sad dog.

We climbed into the boat and lowered the outboard into the water. Becky yanked the starter cord three times and the engine coughed into life and we puttered down the little channel to the sea.

# 17

# individual broccoli tartlets

We ran out of petrol halfway, having used the back-up supply to destroy the Weff-Beam. But there were oars and it was a sunny day, and just being on the surface of our own planet was a pleasure.

I tried to explain everything to Becky, but after a while she told me to stop. 'It's doing my head in, Jimbo. I'm tired and hungry and filthy. I've been living in the wilderness for nearly a week, hitting strange people over the head. I need normal. I need ordinary. I need bacon and fried eggs and toast. And I need a long hot shower. I do not need hover-scooters and intergalactic ferries.'

So she went and sat at the bow and Charlie sat facing me while I rowed and we shared our stories about how he'd been captured and how Becky and I had set off in pursuit on a stolen motorbike.

And maybe Bob-with-the-Hawaiian-shirt was right. Maybe it was cool being on a planet on the far side of the known galaxy. And maybe it was even cooler escaping and getting home again. But the coolest thing of all was having my best friend back.

'What about Mrs Pearce?' I said.

'What do you mean?' asked Charlie.

'She said she was going to make us suffer. You don't think she's going to, like, track us down and kill us, do you?'

Charlie put his head on one side and stared at me. 'She's an elderly lady with no job. The police will be looking for her. She has a tail. And no belly button. If I were her I'd be heading for the hills and living off nuts and berries.'

We took turns rowing and after a couple of hours we reached Elgol Harbour with two seagulls circling above us and a friendly seal in our wake.

The red Volvo was parked a little way up the road from the slipway.

'So,' said Charlie, rubbing his hands together, 'are we going to break in and hotwire it?'

# boom!

'Don't be daft,' said Becky. 'I had the driver tied up for three days.' She fished a set of car keys out of the holdall. 'These were in his pocket.'

'You are a true professional,' said Charlie.

'Thank you,' said Becky.

'Can I have a go at driving?' said Charlie.

'Are you out of your mind?' said Becky. 'Get in the back.'

The Volvo was pretty straightforward after the Moto Guzzi. It had four wheels for starters, so it wasn't going to fall over sideways. We scraped a couple of stone walls and bumped in and out of a few ditches over the first couple of miles but Becky soon got the hang of it.

The journey was glorious. All those things I'd never looked at before seemed wonderful now. Cooling towers. Transit vans. Concrete bridges. I looked at electricity pylons and felt a warm glow in my heart.

After three hours we stopped at Gretna Green. Becky ordered her fry-up, I ordered a pizza and

Charlie ordered a black coffee and four apple turnovers.

We had another six hours of driving in which to plan our stories. But we were too tired. After about four minutes Charlie and I fell asleep and didn't wake up till we reached the M25. Luckily, Becky only fell asleep twice, but each time she was woken up by a lorry honking as she veered into the wrong lane of the motorway.

We offered to drop Charlie off first but he reckoned our parents were less likely to kill him.

When we pulled into the car park by the flats I looked up at the tatty, peeling, weather-stained block and I must admit I got a bit tearful. Then I remembered the complications waiting upstairs and my heart sank.

I turned to Becky. 'What are we going to say?'

'We?' said Becky. 'I think that's your job, mate. But if you want my advice, I'd go easy on the aliens-with-hairy-tails-and-space-travel aspect of the whole thing.'

'Gird your loins,' said Charlie. 'Let's get this over with.'

# boom!

Becky unlocked the door of the flat and we stepped inside. Mum was on the phone. She dropped it and froze for several seconds. Then she screamed. It was actually quite frightening. She threw her arms around me and Becky and squeezed and cried and shouted, 'You're alive! You're alive!'

Then Dad came into the hallway and did the same thing, without the screaming. Then everyone noticed that Charlie was standing to one side looking a bit left out so we grabbed hold of him and had a group hug, by which time all of us were crying, even Charlie, and I'd never seen him cry before, ever.

Things calmed down after a few minutes and we stopped hugging each other. Mum's face went a bit dark and she said, 'Where in God's name have you been?'

And this was the point when I realized we should have worked out a story. 'Well . . .'

There was a horrible silence.

'You disappear for a week,' said Mum, her joy ebbing rapidly away. 'You don't tell us where you're going. We call and you don't ring us back. We've been through hell wondering what happened to you.'

Then Charlie had a brainwave. And I have to say that it was both simple and rather brilliant. 'We were kidnapped.'

'Kidnapped?' said Dad.

'Kidnapped?' said Mum.

'By Mr Kidd,' said Charlie. 'And Mrs Pearce. From school.'

'They took us to Scotland,' I said. 'To Loch Coruisk. On the Isle of Skye.'

'What . . . !?' said Mum. 'What . . . !? What . . . !?' She sounded a bit like a chicken.

'So,' said Dad, shaking his head, 'who wrecked the flat?'

'What?' asked Charlie.

I looked over Dad's shoulder and saw two halves of the snapped coffee table stacked in the corner of the living room and it all came back to me. 'Oh, that,' I said.

'We came back home,' said Dad. 'The fridge was on its side. The sofa was upside down. And we found one of the kitchen chairs in the car park.'

'Obviously we didn't want to be kidnapped,' said Becky, as if this was the most obvious thing in the world. 'So we put up a fight.'

'But . . . but . . . but . . .' said Mum, sounding like a slightly different kind of chicken. 'But why did they kidnap you?'

'I have absolutely no idea,' said Charlie breezily. 'You'll have to ask Mrs Pearce and Mr Kidd. Perhaps they can explain everything.'

# boom!

'I'm going to ring the police,' said Dad.

'Excellent idea,' said Charlie. 'But I really do think I ought to go home first.'

Becky and I showered rapidly and grabbed some clean clothes and Dad drove us all over to Charlie's house.

We knocked on the door and it was pretty much a repeat of what happened at our house. The hugging, the crying. Except that Mrs Brooks screamed a lot louder than Mum.

Dr Brooks rang the police, and two sergeants arrived ten minutes later. Reassuringly, neither of them were wearing brass wristbands.

We told them the kidnapping story. Like Becky suggested, we missed out the aliens-with-hairy-tails-and-space-travel aspect. And the stealing-a-motorbike-and-a-car-and-driving-without-a-licence aspect. And the saving-the-Earth-from-destruction aspect.

The police asked us whether we wanted counselling. We said we'd prefer a hot supper. They told us they'd be in touch and headed out to their car.

Charlie, Becky and I then wandered into the kitchen to discover that Dad and Mrs Brooks had formed a team. Mrs Brooks was rustling up a Stilton sauce to pour over steamed vegetables, while Dad was putting together some individual broccoli tartlets. Mrs Brooks was really rather impressed.

Indeed, while we were eating supper she said that if he was looking for work, she often needed help with some of her bigger catering jobs. Dad said he was very flattered but he'd have to go away and think about it.

Over a dessert of pears in chocolate custard Mum asked Becky whether she was going to ring Craterface. Except she called him Terry because she was in a good mood because we weren't dead. And Becky said she'd be happy if she never saw the lying skunk again. Which was probably just as well since we'd left the Moto Guzzi in Scotland.

Then there was a loud *pop!* and Dr Brooks appeared carrying champagne and a tray of seven glasses. He filled them, we raised them, Dad said, 'Welcome home' and Charlie sank his glass in one go and let out one of the loudest burps I have ever heard in my life.

## 18

# a bunker under the
# brecon beacons

School on Monday morning was particularly excellent. For obvious reasons. When your headmistress stands up in assembly and says you were kidnapped by two of your teachers, but you escaped and they're now on the run from the police, a party atmosphere continues pretty much unabated for the rest of the week.

We were officially cooler than any other pupils in living memory, and I reckoned it was probably a good month before any teacher would feel confident enough to give either of us a detention.

Dad decided to take the job with Charlie's mum. He stuck it for three whole weeks. That was about his limit. She was terrifying, so Dad said. During one particularly stressful wedding reception she did her breadboard-throwing thing. He was inches away from a visit to Accident and Emergency.

Luckily, he was offered a more lucrative and less dangerous job in the Grand Café in town, so he was able to stop working for Mrs Brooks without incurring her everlasting wrath. Even more luckily, the job in the Grand Café was part-time so he was able to come home and cook us beef Wellington and stuffed butternut squash.

The police never came back. I told Charlie something fishy was going on but he told me to chill out and be grateful we weren't taken into custody and injected with truth serum.

So I tried to chill out. And I was doing it really well till we were playing five-a-side football during the lunch break one day a couple of weeks later and I looked across the road and saw a black car with smoked-glass windows parked in front of the laundrette. I didn't tell Charlie. He'd just say I was paranoid.

The following day I saw it when I was standing on the

balcony after supper. It pulled into the car park, idled for a few minutes, then drove away again.

I told Charlie this time. He said I was seeing things. Then we had a class outing to the Science Museum and the black car with the smoked windows was sitting at the side of the street when we got back into the coach. I went a bit crazy at this point. It took Mrs Hennessy a good ten minutes to calm me down and even Charlie said I might have a point.

A few evenings later we met up in the little playground opposite the flats. We sat side by side on the swings. It was getting dark. The orange streetlamps were coming on one by one and the windows in the tower block were lighting up in a chequerboard of different colours.

We were talking about our big secret.

Charlie said, 'Don't you wish you could tell someone? I mean, we could be rich, we could be famous, we could be interviewed by the world's most respected scientists. We could go down in history.' He paused. 'Except of course we wouldn't. Because no one would believe us. We'd probably end up in a psychiatric hospital.'

'Unless we had proof,' I said.

'Yeah,' said Charlie. 'Unless we had proof.'

'Like this, for example,' I said, digging into the back pocket of my jeans and pulling out the floaty balls.

'God,' said Charlie. 'I remember those. Do they still work?'

I placed two of them in the air and let go. They hung there, completely motionless. 'Those are yours,' I said. 'I've got three others. They're, like, a souvenir.'

'Cheers,' said Charlie, sweeping the two balls out of the air and pocketing them.

And that's when I saw the figure emerging from the shadows beneath the trees. My insides froze. 'Charlie . . . ?'

'Oh crap,' he said. 'This is not good, is it?'

I wanted to jump off the swing and run but my legs were no longer taking messages.

The silhouetted figure got closer. 'Hello, James. Hello, Charles.'

It was Mrs Pearce. She was wearing clothes she must have found in a skip. A black plastic raincoat with one sleeve missing. Sandals. Fluorescent-orange workman's trousers. She looked as if she'd washed her hair in engine oil.

# boom!

'You were probably expecting me, weren't you?'

'No,' said Charlie, in a wobbly voice. 'I mean, actually, Jimbo was. But I wasn't.'

'You destroyed my life. You destroyed everything,' she said. 'And do you know what?'

'What?' asked Charlie.

'I have absolutely nothing left to lose.'

'Really?' said Charlie.

I could see now that Mrs Pearce was holding two objects. In her left hand was a large hammer. In her right was a small pointy gardening fork.

'Now hang on,' said Charlie. 'I think we should talk about this. You know, sensibly. Like grown-ups.'

'Shut up,' said Mrs Pearce. 'I'm going to kill you.'

I looked over her shoulder. The black car with the smoked-glass windows was parked in front of the flats. The driver's door was standing open.

'And I'm going to enjoy it so very, very much,' said Mrs Pearce.

There was movement in the darkness behind her. Two more figures were emerging from the trees. Their clothing was dark and their faces were in shadow. But I could see that they were men. Big men.

Mrs Pearce took a couple more steps and raised the hammer above her head. I screamed and fell off the back of the swing and banged my head on the rubberized tarmac. Mrs Pearce lunged and there was a flash of light and a loud *crack!* and she slumped on top of me, the hammer narrowly missing my head.

I pushed her off and struggled to my feet. There was a feathered dart sticking out of her bottom and she was saying, 'Nnnnrrrrgg . . .'

'Gordon Bennett,' said Charlie.

The two men were walking towards us. They had guns. It seemed like a good idea not to run away. The man on the left bent down, yanked the dart out of Mrs Pearce's bottom, rolled her over and fitted her with a black plastic muzzle. The man on the right walked up to us and said, 'Jimbo . . . Charlie . . .'

He held out his hand and we shook it, robotically, unable to do anything else.

'Who are you?' asked Charlie.

'We're the good guys,' said the man. He was wearing a suit but he had an Action Man scar across his cheek and his head was shaved like he'd just returned from a war.

His colleague hoisted Mrs Pearce easily over his shoulder and carried her towards the park gate.

'What's going on?' asked Charlie.

'We reckoned if we stuck close to you she'd show up sooner or later,' said the man. 'Use you as bait.'

'Bait?' I said.

'There's a couple more still at large in the Peak District

but we'll track them down in the next couple of days. I don't think you've got much to worry about.'

Neither Charlie nor I could think of anything to say.

'Well,' said the man, 'we just wanted to thank the two of you. You got there before us. Job well done. We'd give you medals. But medals mean publicity. And we don't like publicity in the department.'

'What department's that?'

The man looked at Charlie as if he were very, very stupid.

'So, um . . .' said Charlie. 'What are you going to do with her? Mrs Pearce, I mean.'

'She'll be in a disused nuclear bunker several hundred metres under the Brecon Beacons.' The man paused. 'Of course, I may be lying.' He held out his hand towards me. 'Floaty balls, please.'

'What?'

'Floaty balls.'

Reluctantly, I slipped my hand into my trouser pocket, took out my three balls and placed them in his hand. He looked over at Charlie. 'Yours too.'

Across the car park I saw his colleague dump Mrs Pearce's unconscious body into the boot of the car, slam it shut, then climb into the driver's seat.

Charlie handed over the final two balls. The man took his hand away and let all five balls hang motionless for a second. 'God, I love these things.' Then he swept them out of the air and slipped them into his jacket pocket.

'What are you going to do now?' asked Charlie nervously. 'Are you, like, going to wipe our brains or something? You know, so we don't remember anything.'

'You've been watching too many films, Charlie. No. It's much simpler than that. If you say anything, to anyone, we track you down and kill you.'

'Right,' said Charlie.

'It's been good meeting you,' said the man. 'I hope you have a pleasant evening.'

He turned and walked through the gate at the edge of the park. He got into the black car with the smoked-glass windows, slammed the door and drove off into the night.